"Are you married?" asked Florence

"No—why do you ask?" Alexander Fitzgibbon smiled very slightly.

"Well, if you were, I don't think we should be going out for dinner like this, without your wife...." She let her words trail off.

"Do I strike you as the kind of man who'd take a girl out while his wife sat at home waiting for him?"

Florence looked sideways at his calm profile. "No."

"That, from someone who is still not sure if she likes me or not, is praise indeed."

Betty Neels is well-known for her romances set in the Netherlands, which is hardly surprising. She married a Dutchman and spent the first twelve years of their marriage living in Holland and working as a nurse. Today, she and her husband make their home in an ancient stone cottage in England's West Country, but they return to Holland often. She loves to explore tiny villages and tour privately owned homes there in order to lend an air of authenticity to the background of her books.

Books by Betty Neels

ROMANTIC ENCOUNTER
Betty Neels

Harlequin Books

TORONTO • NEW YORK • LONDON
AMSTERDAM • PARIS • SYDNEY • HAMBURG
STOCKHOLM • ATHENS • TOKYO • MILAN
MADRID • WARSAW • BUDAPEST • AUCKLAND

Original hardcover edition published in 1992
by Mills & Boon Limited

ISBN 0-373-03249-8

Harlequin Romance first edition February 1993

ROMANTIC ENCOUNTER

CHAPTER ONE

FLORENCE, cleaning the upstairs windows of the vicarage, heard the car coming up the lane and, when it slowed, poked her head over the top sash to see whom it might be. The elegant dark grey Rolls-Royce, sliding to a halt before her father's front door, was unexpected enough to cause her to lean her splendid person even further out of the window so that she might see who was in it. The passenger got out and she recognised him at once. Mr Wilkins, the consultant surgeon she had worked for before she had left the hospital in order to look after her mother and run the house until she was well again—a lengthy business of almost a year. Perhaps he had come to see if she was ready to return to her ward; unlikely, though, for it had been made clear to her that her post would be filled and she would have to take her chance at getting whatever was offered if she wanted to go to work at Colbert's again; besides, a senior consultant wouldn't come traipsing after a ward sister...

The driver of the car was getting out, a very tall, large man with pepper and salt hair. He stood for a moment, looking around him, waiting for Mr Wilkins to join him, and then looked up at her. His air of amused surprise sent her back inside again, banging her head as she went, but she was forced to lean out again when Mr Wilkins caught sight of her and called up to her to come down and let them in.

There was no time to do more than wrench the clean duster off her fiery hair. She went down to the hall and opened the door.

Mr Wilkins greeted her jovially. 'How are you after all these months?' he enquired; he eyed the apron bunched over an elderly skirt and jumper. 'I do hope we haven't called at an inconvenient time?'

Florence's smile was frosty. 'Not at all, sir, we are spring-cleaning.'

Mr Wilkins, who lived in a house with so many gadgets that it never needed spring-cleaning, looked interested. 'Are you really? But you'll spare us a moment to talk, I hope? May I introduce Mr Fitzgibbon?' He turned to his companion. 'This is Florence Napier.'

She offered a rather soapy hand and had it engulfed in his large one. His, 'How do you do?' was spoken gravely, but she felt that he was amused again, and no wonder—she must look a fright.

Which, of course, she did, but a beautiful fright; nothing could dim the glory of her copper hair, tied back carelessly with a boot-lace, and nothing could detract from her lovely face and big blue eyes with their golden lashes. She gave him a cool look and saw that his eyes were grey and intent, so she looked away quickly and addressed herself to Mr Wilkins.

'Do come into the drawing-room. Mother's in the garden with the boys, and Father's writing his sermon. Would you like to have some coffee?'

She ushered them into the big, rather shabby room, its windows open on to the mild April morning. 'Do sit down,' she begged them. 'I'll let Mother know that you're here and fetch in the coffee.'

'It is you we have come to see, Florence,' said Mr Wilkins.

'Me? Oh, well—all the same, I'm sure Mother will want to meet you.'

She opened the old-fashioned window wide and jumped neatly over the sill with the unselfconsciousness of a child, and Mr Fitzgibbon's firm mouth twitched at the corners. 'She's very professional on the ward,' observed Mr Wilkins, 'and very neat. Of course, if she's cleaning the house I suppose she gets a little untidy.'

Mr Fitzgibbon agreed blandly and then stood up as Florence returned, this time with her mother and using the door. Mrs Napier was small and slim and pretty, and still a little frail after her long illness. Florence made the introductions, settled her mother in a chair and went away to make the coffee.

'Oo's that, then?' asked Mrs Buckett, who came up twice a week from the village to do the rough, and after years of faithful service considered herself one of the family.

'The surgeon I worked for at Colbert's—and he's brought a friend with him.'

'What for?'

'I've no idea. Be a dear and put the kettle on while I lay a tray. I'll let you know as soon as I can find out.'

While the kettle boiled she took off her apron, tugged the jumper into shape and poked at her hair. 'Not that it matters,' she told Mrs Buckett. 'I looked an absolute frump when they arrived.'

'Go on with yer, love—you couldn't look a frump if you tried. Only yer could wash yer 'ands.'

Florence had almost decided that she didn't like Mr Fitzgibbon, but she had to admit that his manners were nice. He got up and took the tray from her and didn't sit down again until she was sitting herself. His bedside manner would be impeccable...

They drank their coffee and made small talk, but not for long. Her mother put her cup down and got to her feet. 'Mr Wilkins tells me that he wants to talk to you, Florence, and I would like to go back to the garden and see what the boys are doing with the cold frame.'

She shook hands and went out of the room, and they all sat down again.

'Your mother is well enough for you to return to work, Florence?'

'Yes. Dr Collins saw her a few days ago. I must find someone to come in for an hour or two each day, but I must find a job first.' She saw that Mr Wilkins couldn't see the sense of that, but Mr Fitzgibbon had understood at once, although he didn't speak.

'Yes, yes, of course,' said Mr Wilkins briskly. 'Well, I've nothing for you, I'm afraid, but Mr Fitzgibbon has.'

'I shall need a nurse at my consulting-rooms in two weeks' time. I mentioned it to Mr Wilkins, and he remembered you and assures me that you would suit me very well.'

What about you suiting me? reflected Florence, and went a little pink because he was staring at her in that amused fashion again, reading her thoughts. 'I don't know anything about that sort of nursing,' she said, 'I've always worked in hospital; I'm not sure——'

'Do not imagine that the job is a sinecure. I have a large practice and I operate in a number of hospitals, specialising in chest surgery. My present nurse accompanies me and scrubs for the cases, but perhaps you don't feel up to that?'

'I've done a good deal of Theatre work, Mr Fitzgibbon,' said Florence, nettled.

'In that case, I think that you might find the job interesting. You would be free at the weekends, although

I should warn you that I am occasionally called away at such times and you would need to hold yourself in readiness to accompany me. My rooms are in Wimpole Street, and Sister Brice has lodgings close by. I suppose you might take them over if they suited you. As to salary...'

He mentioned a sum which caused her pretty mouth to drop open.

'That's a great deal more——'

'Of course it is; you would be doing a great deal more work and your hours will have to fit in with mine.'

'This nurse who is leaving,' began Florence.

'To get married.' His voice was silky. 'She has been with me for five years.' He gave her a considered look. 'Think it over and let me know. I'll give you a ring tomorrow—shall we say around three o'clock?'

She had the strong feeling that if she demurred at that he would still telephone then, and expect her to answer, too. 'Very well, Mr Fitzgibbon,' she said in a non-committal voice, at the same time doing rapid and rather inaccurate sums in her head; the money would be a godsend—there would be enough to pay for extra help at the vicarage, they needed a new set of saucepans, and the washing-machine had broken down again...

She bade the two gentlemen goodbye, smiling nicely at Mr Wilkins, whom she liked, and giving Mr Fitzgibbon a candid look as she shook hands. He was very good-looking, with a high-bridged nose and a determined chin and an air of self-possession. He didn't smile as he said goodbye.

Not an easy man to get to know, she decided, watching the Rolls sweep through the vicarage gate.

When she went back indoors her mother had come in from the garden.

'He looked rather nice,' she observed, obviously following a train of thought. 'Why did he come, Florence?'

'He wants a nurse for his practice—a private one, I gather. Mr Wilkins recommended me.'

'How kind, darling. Just at the right moment, too. It will save you hunting around the hospitals and places...'

'I haven't said I'd take it, Mother.'

'Why not, love? I'm very well able to take over the household again—is the pay very bad?'

'It's very generous. I'd have to live in London, but I'd be free every weekend unless I was wanted—Mr Fitzgibbon seems to get around everywhere rather a lot; he specialises in chest surgery.'

'Did Mr Wilkins offer you your old job back, darling?'

'No. There's nothing for me at Colbert's...'

'Then, Florence, you must take this job. It will make a nice change and you'll probably meet nice people.' It was one of Mrs Napier's small worries that her beautiful daughter seldom met men—young men, looking for a wife—after all, she was five and twenty and, although the housemen at the hospital took her out, none of them, as far as she could make out, was of the marrying kind—too young and no money. Now, a nice older man, well established and able to give Florence all the things she had had to do without... Mrs Napier enjoyed a brief daydream.

'Is he married?' she asked.

'I have no idea, Mother. I should think he might be—I mean, he's not a young man, is he?' Florence, collecting coffee-cups, wasn't very interested. 'I'll talk to Father. It might be a good idea if I took the job for a time until there's a vacancy at Colbert's or one of the top teaching hospitals. I don't want to get out of date.'

'Go and talk to your father now, dear.' Mrs Napier glanced at the clock. 'Either by now he's finished his sermon, or he's got stuck. He'll be glad of the interruption.'

Mr Napier, when appealed to, giving the matter grave thought, decided that Florence would be wise to take the job. 'I do not know this Mr Fitzgibbon,' he observed, 'but if he is known to Mr Wilkins he must be a dependable sort of chap! The salary is a generous one too... not that you should take that into consideration, Florence, if you dislike the idea.'

She didn't point out that the salary was indeed a consideration. With the boys at school and then university, the vicar's modest stipend had been whittled down to its minimum so that there would be money enough for their future. The vicar, a kind, good man, ready to give the coat off his back to anyone in need, was nevertheless blind to broken-down washing-machines, worn-out sauce-pans and the fact that his wife hadn't had a new hat for more than a year.

'I like the idea, Father,' said Florence robustly, 'and I can come home at the weekend too. I'll go and see Miss Payne in the village and arrange for her to come in for an hour or so each day to give Mother a hand. Mrs Buckett can't do everything. I'll pay—it is really a very generous salary.'

'Will you be able to keep yourself in comfort, Florence?'

She assured him that she could perfectly well do that. 'And the lodgings his present nurse has will be vacant if I'd like to take them.'

'It sounds most suitable,' said her father, 'but you must, of course, do what you wish, my dear.'

She wasn't at all sure what she did wish but she had plenty of common sense; she needed to get a job and start earning money again, and she had, by some lucky chance, been offered one without any effort on her part.

When Mr Fitzgibbon telephoned the following day, precisely at three o'clock, and asked her in his cool voice if she had considered his offer, she accepted in a voice as cool as his own.

He didn't say that he was pleased. 'Then perhaps you will come up to town very shortly and talk to Sister Brice. Would next Monday be convenient—in the early afternoon?'

'There is a train from Sherborne just after ten o'clock—I could be at your rooms about one o'clock.'

'That will suit Sister Brice very well. You have the address and the telephone number.'

'Yes, thanks.'

His, 'Very well, goodbye, Miss Napier,' was abrupt, even if uttered politely.

The Reverend Napier, his sermon written and nothing but choir practice to occupy him, drove Florence into Sherborne to catch the morning train. Gussage Tollard was a mere four miles to that town as the crow flew, but, taking into account the elderly Austin and the winding lanes, turning and twisting every hundred yards or so, the distance by car was considerably more.

'Be sure and have a good lunch,' advised her father. 'One can always get a good meal at Lyons.'

Florence said that she would; her father went to London so rarely that he lived comfortably in the past as regarded cafés, bus queues and the like, and she had no intention of disillusioning him.

She bade him goodbye at the station, assured him that she would be on the afternoon train from Waterloo, and was borne away to London.

She had a cup of coffee and a sandwich at Waterloo Station and queued for a bus, got off at Oxford Circus, and, since she had a little time to spare, looked at a few shops along Oxford Street before turning off towards Wimpole Street. The houses were dignified Regency, gleaming with pristine paintwork and shining brass plates. Number eighty-seven would be halfway down, she decided, and wondered where the lodgings were that she might take over. It was comparatively quiet here and the sun was shining; after the bustle and the noise of Oxford Street it was peaceful—as peaceful as one could be in London, she amended, thinking of Gussage Tollard, which hadn't caught up with the modern world yet, and a good thing too.

Mr Fitzgibbon, standing at the window of his consulting-room, his hands in his pockets, watched her coming along the pavement below. With a view to the sobriety of the occasion, she had shrouded a good deal of her brilliant hair under a velvet cap which matched the subdued tones of her French navy jacket and skirt. She was wearing her good shoes too; they pinched a little, but that was in a good cause...

She glanced up as she reached the address she had been given, to see Mr Fitzgibbon staring down at her, unsmiling. He looked out of temper, and she stared back before mounting the few steps to the front door and ringing the bell. The salary he had offered was good, she reflected, but she had a nasty feeling that he would be a hard master.

The door was opened by an elderly porter, who told her civilly that Mr Fitzgibbon's consulting-rooms were

on the first floor and would she go up? Once on the
landing above there was another door with its highly
polished bell, this time opened by a cosily plump middle-
aged lady who said in a friendly voice, 'Ah, here you
are. I'm Mr Fitzgibbon's receptionist—Mrs Keane.
You're to go straight in...'

'I was to see Sister Brice,' began Florence.

'Yes, dear, and so you shall. But Mr Fitzgibbon wants
to see you now.' She added in an almost reverent voice,
'He should be going to his lunch, but he decided to see
you first.'

Florence thought of several answers to this but uttered none of them; she needed the job too badly.

Mr Fitzgibbon had left the window and was sitting
behind his desk. He got up as Mrs Keane showed her in
and wished her a cool, 'Good afternoon, Miss Napier,'
and begged her to take a seat. Once she was sitting he
was in no haste to speak.

Finally he said, 'Sister Brice is at lunch; she will show
you exactly what your duties will be. I suggest that you
come on a month's trial, and after that period I would
ask you to give three months' notice should you wish to
leave. I dislike changing my staff.'

'You may not wish me to stay after a month,' Florence
pointed out in a matter-of-fact voice.

'There is that possibility. That can be discussed at the
end of the month. You are agreeable to your working
conditions? I must warn you that this is not a nine-to-
five job; your personal life is of no interest to me, but
on no account must it infringe upon your work here. I
depend upon the loyalty of my staff.'

She was tempted to observe that at the salary she was
being offered she was unlikely to be disloyal. She said
forthrightly, 'I'm free to do what I like and work where

I wish; I like to go to my home whenever I can, but otherwise I have no other interests.'

'No prospects of marriage?'

She opened her beautiful eyes wide. 'Since you ask, no.'

'I'm surprised. I should like you to start—let me see; Sister Brice leaves at the end of next week, a Saturday. Perhaps you will get settled in on the Sunday and start work here on the Monday morning.'

'That will suit me very well.' She did hide a smile at his surprised look; he was probably used to having things his own way. 'Will it be possible for me to see the rooms I am to have?'

He said impatiently, 'Yes, yes, why not? Sister Brice can take you there. Are you spending the night in town?'

'No, I intend to go back on the five o'clock train from Waterloo.'

There was a knock on the door and he called 'come in', and Sister Brice put her head round the door and said cheerfully, 'Shall I take over, sir?' She came into the room and shook Florence's hand.

The phone rang and Mr Fitzgibbon lifted the receiver. 'Yes, please. There's no one until three o'clock, is there? I shall want you here then.'

He glanced at Florence. 'Goodbye, Miss Napier; I expect to see you a week on Monday morning.'

Sister Brice closed the door gently behind them. 'He's marvellous to work for; you mustn't take any notice of his abruptness.'

'I shan't,' said Florence. 'Where do we start?'

The consulting-rooms took up the whole of the first floor. Besides Mr Fitzgibbon's room and the waiting-room, there was a very small, well-equipped dressing-room, an examination-room leading from the con-

sulting-room, a cloakroom and a tiny kitchen. 'He likes
his coffee around ten o'clock, but if he has a lot of patients he'll not stop. We get ours when we can. I get here
about eight o'clock—the first patient doesn't get here
before half-past nine, but everything has to be quite
ready. Mr Fitzgibbon quite often goes to the hospital
first and takes a look at new patients there; he goes back
there around noon or one o'clock and we have our lunch
and tidy up and so on, he comes back here about four
o'clock unless he's operating, and he sees patients until
half-past five. You do Theatre, don't you? He always
has the same theatre sister at Colbert's, but if he's operating at another hospital, doesn't matter where, he'll
take you with him to scrub.'

'Another hospital in London?'

'Could be; more often than not it's Birmingham or
Edinburgh or Bristol—I've been to Brussels several times,
the Middle East, and a couple of times to Berlin.'

'I can't speak German...'

Sister Brice laughed. 'You don't need to—he does all
the talking; you just carry on as though you were at
Colbert's. He did mention that occasionally you have to
miss a weekend? It's made up to you, though.' She
opened a cupboard with a key from her pocket. 'I've
been very happy here and I shall miss the work, but it's
a full-time job and there's not much time over from it,
certainly not if one is married.' She was pulling out
drawers. 'There's everything he needs for operating—he
likes his own instruments and it's your job to see that
they're all there and ready. They get put in this bag.'

She glanced at her watch. 'There's time to go over to
my room; you can meet Mrs Twist and see if it'll suit
you. She gets your breakfast and cooks high tea about
half-past six. There's a washing-machine and a tele-

phone you may use. She doesn't encourage what she calls gentlemen friends...'

'I haven't got any...'

'You're pretty enough to have half a dozen, if you don't mind my saying so.'

'Thank you. I think I must be hard to please.'

Mrs Twist lived in one of the narrow streets behind Wimpole Street, not five minutes' walk away. The house was small, one of a row, but it was very clean and neat, rather like Mrs Twist—small, too, and bony with pepper and salt hair and a printed cotton pinny. She eyed Florence shrewdly with small blue eyes and led her upstairs to a room overlooking the street, nicely furnished. 'Miss Brice 'as her breakfast downstairs, quarter to eight sharp,' she observed, 'the bathroom's across the landing, there's a machine for yer smalls and yer can 'ang them out in the back garden. I'll cook a meal at half-past six of an evening, something 'ot; if I'm out it'll be in the oven. Me and Miss Brice 'as never 'ad a cross word and I 'opes we'll get on as nicely.'

'Well, I hope so too, Mrs Twist. This is a very nice room and I'm sure I shall appreciate a meal each evening. You must let me know if there's anything——'

'Be sure I will, Miss Napier; I'm one for speaking out, but Mr Fitzgibbon told me you was a sensible, quiet-spoken young lady, and what 'e says I'll believe.'

Sister Brice was waiting downstairs in the prim front room. 'There's time to go back for half an hour,' she pointed out. 'I'm ready for the first patient; Mr Fitzgibbon won't be back until just before three o'clock, and Mrs Keane will already have got the notes out.'

They bade Mrs Twist goodbye and walked back to Wimpole Street, where Mrs Keane was putting on the kettle. Over cups of tea she and Sister Brice covered the bare bones of Mr Fitzgibbon's information with a wealth of their own, so that by the time Florence left she had a sound idea of what she might expect. Nothing like having a ward in the hospital, she reflected on her way to the station. She would have to make her own routine and keep to it as much as possible, allowing for Mr Fitzgibbon's demands upon her time. All the same, she thought that she would like it; she was answerable to no one but herself and him, of course—her bedsitter was a good deal better than she had expected it to be, and there was the added bonus of going home each weekend. She spent the return journey doing sums on the back of an envelope, and alighted at Sherborne knowing that the saucepans and washing-machine need no longer be pipe-dreams. At the end of the month they would be installed in the vicarage kitchen. What was more, she would be able to refurbish her spring wardrobe.

'Mr Fitzgibbon seems to be an employer of the highest order,' observed her father when she recounted the day's doings to him.

She agreed, but what sort of a man was he? she wondered; she still wasn't sure if she liked him or not.

She spent the next two weeks in a burst of activity; the spring-cleaning had to be finished, a lengthy job in the rambling vicarage, and someone had to be found who would come each day for an hour or so. Mrs Buckett was a splendid worker but, although Mrs Napier was very nearly herself once more, there were tiresome tasks—the ironing, the shopping and the cooking—to be dealt with. Miss Payne, in the village, who had recently lost her very old mother, was only too glad to fill the post for a modest sum.

Florence packed the clothes she decided she would need, added one or two of her more precious books and a batch of family photos to grace the little mantelpiece in her bedsitter, and, after a good deal of thought, a long skirt and top suitable for an evening out. It was unlikely that she would need them, but one never knew. When she had been at the hospital she had never lacked invitations from various members of the medical staff—usually a cinema and coffee and sandwiches on the way home, occasionally a dinner in some popular restaurant—but she had been at home now for nearly a year and she had lost touch. She hadn't minded; she was country born and bred and she hadn't lost her heart to anyone. Occasionally she remembered that she was twenty-five and there was no sign of the man Mrs Buckett coyly described as Mr Right. Florence had the strong suspicion that Mrs Buckett's Mr Right and her own idea of him were two quite different people.

She left home on the Sunday evening and, when it came to the actual moment of departure, with reluctance. The boys had gone back to school and she wouldn't see them again until half-term, but there was the Sunday school class she had always taken for her father, choir practice, the various small duties her mother had had to give up while she had been ill, and there was Charlie Brown, the family cat, and Higgins, the elderly Labrador dog; she had become fond of them during her stay at home.

'I'll be home next weekend,' she told her mother bracingly, 'and I'll phone you this evening.' All the same, the sight of her father's elderly greying figure waving from the platform as the train left made her feel childishly forlorn.

Mrs Twist's home dispelled some of her feelings of strangeness. There was a tray of tea waiting for her in her room and the offer of help if she should need it.

'And there is a bite of supper at eight o'clock, it being Sunday,' said Mrs Twist, 'and just this once you can use the phone downstairs. There's a phone box just across the road that Miss Brice used.'

Florence unpacked, arranged the photos and her bits and pieces, phoned her mother to assure her in a cheerful voice that she had settled in nicely and everything was fine, and then went down to her supper.

'Miss Brice was away for most weekends,' said the landlady, 'but sometimes she 'ad ter work, so we had a bite together.'

So Florence ate her supper in the kitchen with Mrs Twist and listened to that lady's comments upon her neighbours, the cost of everything and her bad back. 'Miss Brice told Mr Fitzgibbon about it,' she confided, 'and he was ever so kind—sent me to the 'ospital with a special note to a friend of 'is. 'E's ever so nice; you'll like working for him.'

'Oh, I'm sure I will,' said Florence, secretly not at all sure about it.

She arrived at the consulting-rooms well before time in the morning. A taciturn elderly man opened the door to her, nodded when she told him who she was, and went to unlock Mr Fitzgibbon's own door. The place had been hoovered and dusted and there were fresh flowers in the vase on the coffee-table. Presumably Mr Fitzgibbon had a fairy godmother who waved her wand and summoned cleaning ladies at unearthly hours. She went through to the cloakroom and found her white uniform laid out for her; there was a frilled muslin cap too. He didn't agree with the modern version of a nurse's uniform, and she registered approval as she changed. She clasped her navy belt with its silver buckle round her neat waist and began a cautious survey of the premises, peering in cupboards and drawers, making sure where everything was; Mr Fitzgibbon wasn't a man to suffer fools gladly, she was sure, and she had no intention of being caught out.

Mrs Keane arrived next, begged Florence to put on the kettle and sorted out the notes of the patients who were expected. 'Time for a cup of tea,' she explained. 'We'll be lucky if we get time for coffee this morning—there's old Lady Trump coming, and even if we allow her twice as long as anyone else she always holds everything up. There's the phone, dear; answer it, will you?'

Mr Fitzgibbon's voice, unflurried, sounded in her ear. 'I shall be about fifteen minutes late. Is Sister Napier there yet?'

'Yes,' said Florence, slightly tartly, 'she is; she came at eight o'clock sharp.'

'The time we agreed upon?' he asked silkily. 'I should warn you that I frown upon unpunctuality.'

'In that case, Mr Fitzgibbon,' said Florence sweetly, 'why don't you have one of those clocking-in machines installed?'

'I frown on impertinence too,' said Mr Fitzgibbon, and hung up.

Mrs Keane had been listening; she didn't say anything but went and made the tea and sat down opposite Florence in the tiny kitchen. 'I'll tell you about the patients coming this morning. One new case—a Mr Willoughby. He's a CA, left lobe, sent to us by his doctor. Lives somewhere in the Midlands—retired. The other three are back for check-ups—Lady Trump first; allow half an hour for her, and she needs a lot of help getting undressed and dressed and so on. Then there is little Miss Powell, who had a lobectomy two months ago, and the last one is a child, Susie Castle—seven years old—

a fibrocystic. It's not for me to say, but I think it's a losing battle. Such a dear child, too.'

She glanced at the clock. 'He'll be here in about two minutes...'

She was right; Mr Fitzgibbon came in quietly, wished them good morning and went to his consulting-room.

'Take Mr Willoughby in,' hissed Mrs Keane, 'and stand on the right side of the door. Mr Fitzgibbon will nod when he wants you to show the patient into the examination-room. If it's a man you go back into the consulting-room unless he asks you to stay.'

Florence adjusted her cap just so and took herself off to the waiting-room in time to receive Mr Willoughby, a small, meek man, who gave the impression that he had resigned himself to his fate. An opinion not shared by Mr Fitzgibbon, however. Florence, watching from her corner, had to allow that his quiet assured air convinced his patient that it was by no means hopeless.

'This is a fairly common operation,' he said soothingly, 'and there is no reason why you shouldn't live a normal life for some years to come. Now, Sister will show you the examination-room, and I'll take a look. Your own doctor seems to agree with me, and I think that you should give yourself a chance.'

So Florence led away a more hopeful Mr Willoughby, informed Mr Fitzgibbon that his patient was ready for him, and retired discreetly to the consulting-room.

Upon their return Mr Fitzgibbon said, 'Ah, Sister, will you hand Mr Willoughby over to Mrs Keane, please?' He shook hands with his patient and Florence led him away, a much happier man than when he had come in.

Lady Trump was quite a different matter. A lady in her eighties, who, at Mr Fitzgibbon's behest, had undergone successful surgery and had taken on a new lease of life; moreover, she was proud of the fact and took a good deal of pleasure in boring her family and friends with all the details of her recovery...

'You're new,' she observed, eyeing Florence through old-fashioned gold-rimmed pince-nez.

'Sister Brice is getting married.'

'Hmm—I'm surprised you aren't married yourself.'

Ushered into the consulting-room, where she shook hands with Mr Fitzgibbon, she informed him, 'Well, you won't keep this gel long, she's far too pretty.'

His cold eyes gave Florence's person a cursory glance. His, 'Indeed,' was uttered with complete uninterest. 'Well, Lady Trump, how have you been since I saw you last?'

Mrs Keane had been right: the old lady took twice as long as anyone else. Besides, she had got on all the wrong clothes; she must have known that she would be examined, yet she was wearing a dress with elaborate fastenings, tiny buttons running from her neck to her waist, and under that a series of petticoats and camisoles, all of which had to be removed to an accompaniment of warnings as to how it should be done. When at last Florence ushered her back to Mrs Keane's soothing care, she breathed a sigh of relief.

'Would you like your coffee, sir?' she asked, hoping that he would say yes so that she might swallow a mug herself. 'Miss Powell hasn't arrived yet.'

'Yes,' said Mr Fitzgibbon without lifting his handsome head from his notes, 'and have one yourself.'

Miss Powell was small and thin and mouse-like, and he treated her with a gentle kindness Florence was surprised to see. The little lady went away presently, reassured as to her future, and Florence, at Mr Fitzgibbon's brisk bidding, ushered in little Susie Castle and her mother.

Susie was small for her age and wore a look of elderly resignation, which Florence found heart-rending, but even if she looked resigned she was full of life just as any healthy child, and it was obvious that she and Mr Fitzgibbon were on the best of terms. He teased her gently and made no effort to stop her when she picked up his pen and began to draw on the big notepad on his desk.

'How about a few days in hospital, Susie?' he wanted to know. 'Then I'll have time to come and see you every day; we might even find time for a game of draughts or dominoes.'

'Why?'

'Well, it's so much easier for me to look after you there. We'll go to X-ray...'

'You'll be there with me? It's always a bit dark.'

'I'll be there. Shall we have a date?'

Susie giggled. 'All right.' She put out a small hand, and Florence, who was nearest, took it in hers. The child studied her face for a moment.

'You're very pretty. Haven't you met Prince Charming yet?'

'Not yet, but I expect I shall one day soon.' Florence squeezed the small hand. 'Will you be my bridesmaid?'

'Yes, of course; who do you want to marry? Mr Fitzgibbon?'

Her mother made a small sound—an apology—but Florence laughed. 'My goodness, no... Now, supposing we get you dressed again so that you can go home.'

It was later that day, after the afternoon patients had gone and she was clearing up the examination-room and putting everything ready for the next day, that Mr Fitzgibbon, on his way home, paused beside her.

'You are happy with your work, Miss Napier?'

'Yes, thank you, sir. I like meeting people...'

'Let us hope that you meet your Prince Charming soon,' he observed blandly, and shut the door quietly behind him.

Leaving her wondering if he was already looking forward to the day when she would want to leave.

CHAPTER TWO

THE days passed quickly; Mr Fitzgibbon allowed few idle moments in his day, and Florence quickly discovered that he didn't expect her to have any either. By the end of the week she had fallen into a routine of sorts, but a very flexible one, for on two evenings she had returned to the consulting-rooms to attend those patients who were unable or who didn't wish to come during the day, and on one afternoon she had been whisked at a moment's notice to a large nursing home to scrub for the biopsy he wished to perform on one of his patients there. The theatre there had been adequate, but only just, and she had acquitted herself well enough. On the way back to his rooms she had asked if he performed major surgery there.

'Good lord, no; biopsies, anything minor, but otherwise they come into Colbert's or one of the big private hospitals.'

They had already established a satisfactory working relationship by the end of the week, but she was no nearer to knowing anything about him than on the first occasion of their meeting. He came and went, leaving telephone numbers for her in case he should be needed, but never mentioning where he was going. His home, for all she knew, might be the moon. As for him, he made no attempt to get to know her either. He had enquired if she was comfortable at Mrs Twist's house, and if she found the work within her scope—a question which ruffled her calm considerably—and told her at the end

of the week that she was free to go home for the weekend
if she wished. But not, she discovered, on the Friday
evening. The last patient didn't leave until six o'clock;
she had missed her train and the next one too, and the
one after that would get her to Sherborne too late, and
she had no intention of keeping her father out of his
bed in order to meet the train.

She bade Mr Fitzgibbon goodnight, and when he
asked, 'You're going home, Miss Napier?' she answered
rather tartly that yes, but in the morning by an early
train. To which he answered nothing, only gave her a
thoughtful look. She had reached the door when he said,
'You will be back on Sunday evening all right? We shall
need to be ready on Monday morning soon after nine
o'clock.' With which she had to be content.

It was lovely to be home again. In the kitchen, drinking
coffee while her mother sat at the kitchen table, scraping
carrots, and Mrs Buckett hovered, anxious not to miss
a word, Florence gave a faithful account of her week.

'Do you like working for Mr Fitzgibbon?' asked her
mother.

'Oh, yes, he has a very large practice and beds at
Colbert's, and he seems to be much in demand for
consultations...'

'Is he married?' asked Mrs Napier artlessly.

'I haven't the slightest idea, Mother; in fact, I don't
know a thing about him, and he's not the kind of person
you would ask.'

'Of course, darling—I just wondered if his receptionist or someone who works for him had mentioned
something...'

'The people who work for him never mention him
unless it's something to do with work. Probably they're
not told or are sworn to secrecy...'

'How very interesting,' observed her mother.

The weekend went too swiftly; Florence dug the garden, walked Higgins and sang in the choir on Sunday, made a batch of cakes for the Mothers' Union tea party to be held during the following week, and visited as many of her friends as she had time for. Sunday evening came much too soon, and she got into the train with reluctance. Once she was back in Mrs Twist's house, eating the supper that good lady had ready for her, she found herself looking forward to the week ahead. Her work was by no means dull, and she enjoyed the challenge of not knowing what each day might offer.

Monday offered nothing special. She was disconcerted to find Mr Fitzgibbon at his desk when she arrived in the morning. He wished her good morning civilly enough and picked up his pen again with a dismissive nod.

'You've been up half the night,' said Florence matter-of-factly, taking in his tired unshaven face, elderly trousers and high-necked sweater. 'I'll make you some coffee.'

She swept out of the room, closing the door gently as she went, put on the kettle and ladled instant coffee into a mug, milked and sugared it lavishly and, with a tin of Rich Tea biscuits, which she and Mrs Keane kept for their elevenses, bore the tray back to the consulting-room.

'There,' she said hearteningly, 'drink that up. The first patient isn't due until half-past nine; you go home and get tidied up. It's a check-up, isn't it? I dare say she'll be late—a name like Witherington-Pugh...'

Mr Fitzgibbon gave a crack of laughter. 'I don't quite see the connection, but yes, she is always unpunctual.'

'There you are, then,' said Florence comfortably. 'Now drink up and go home. You might even have time for a quick nap.'

Mr Fitzgibbon drank his coffee meekly, trying to remember when last anyone had ordered him to drink his coffee and get off home. His childhood probably, he thought sleepily with suddenly vivid memories of Nanny standing over him while he swallowed hot milk.

Rather to his own surprise, he did as he was told, and when Florence went back to the consulting-room with the first batch of notes he had gone. He was back at half-past nine, elegant in a dark grey suit and richly sombre tie, betraying no hint of an almost sleepless night. Indeed, he looked ten years younger, and Florence, eyeing him covertly, wondered how old he was.

Mrs Witherington-Pugh, who had had open chest surgery for an irretractable hernia some years previously, had come for her annual check-up and was as tiresome as Florence had felt in her bones she would be. She was slender to the point of scragginess and swathed in vague, floating garments that took a long time to remove and even longer to put back on. She kept up what Florence privately thought of as a 'poor little me' conversation, and fluttered her artificial eyelashes at Mr Fitzgibbon, who remained unmoved. He pronounced her well, advised her to take more exercise, eat plenty and take up some interest.

'But I dare not eat more than a few mouthfuls,' declared the lady. 'I'm not one of your strapping young women who needs three meals a day.' Her eyes strayed to Florence's Junoesque person. 'If one is well built, of course...'

Florence composed her beautiful features into a calm she didn't feel and avoided Mr Fitzgibbon's eye. 'None the less,' he observed blandly, 'you should eat sensibly; the slenderness of youth gives way to the thinness of middle age, you know.'

Mrs Witherington-Pugh simpered. 'Well, I don't need to worry too much about that for some years yet,' she told him.

Mr Fitzgibbon merely smiled pleasantly and shook her hand.

Florence tidied up and he sat and watched her. 'Bring in Sir Percival Watts,' he said finally. He glanced at his watch. 'We're running late. I shan't need you for ten minutes—go and have your coffee. I'll have mine before the next patient——' he glanced at the pile of notes before him '—Mr Simpson. His tests are back; he'll need surgery.' He didn't look up as she went out of the room.

Sir Percival was on the point of going when she returned, and she ushered in Mr Simpson; at a nod from Mr Fitzgibbon she busied herself in the examination-room while he talked to his patient. She could hear the murmur of their voices and then silence, and she turned to find Mr Fitzgibbon leaning against the door-frame, watching her.

'I'll be at Colbert's if I'm wanted; I'll be back here about two o'clock. You should be able to leave on time this evening. I expect you go out in the evenings when you're free?'

'Me? No, I've nowhere to go—not on my own, that is. Most of my friends at Colbert's have left or got married; besides, by the time I've had supper there's not much of the evening left.'

'I told you the hours were erratic. Take the afternoon off tomorrow, will you? I shall be operating at Colbert's, and Sister will scrub for me. I shall want you here at six o'clock in the evening—there's a new patient coming to see me.'

He wandered away, and Florence muttered, 'And not one single "please"...'

Save for necessary talk concerning patients that afternoon, he had nothing to say to her, and his goodnight was curt. He must be tired, Florence reflected, watching from the window as he crossed the pavement to his car. She hoped that his wife would be waiting for him with a well-cooked dinner. She glanced at her watch: it was early for dinner, so perhaps he would have high tea; he was such a very large man that he would need plenty of good, nourishing food. She began to arrange a menu in her mind—soup, a roast with plenty of baked potatoes and fresh vegetables, and a fruit pie for afters. Rhubarb, she mused; they had had rhubarb pie at home at the weekend with plenty of cream. Probably his wife didn't do the cooking—he must have a sizeable income from his practice as well as the work he did at the hospital, so there would be a cook and someone to do the housework. Her nimble fingers arranged everything ready for the morning while she added an au pair or a nanny for his children. Two boys and a girl... Mrs Keane's voice aroused her from her musings.

'Are you ready to leave, Florence? It's been a nice easy day, hasn't it? There's someone booked for tomorrow evening...'

Florence went to change out of her uniform. 'Yes, Mr Fitzgibbon's given me the afternoon off, but I have to come back at six o'clock.'

'Ah, yes—did he tell you who it was? No? Forgot, I expect. A very well-known person in the theatre world. Using her married name, of course.' Mrs Keane was going around, checking shut windows and doors. 'Very highly strung,' she commented, for still, despite her years of working for Mr Fitzgibbon, she adhered to the picturesque and sometimes inaccurate medical terms of her youth.

Florence, racing out of her uniform and into a skirt and sweater, envisaged a beautiful not-so-young actress who smoked too much and had developed a nasty cough...

The next day brought its quota of patients in the morning and, since the last of them went around noon, she cleared up and then was free to go. 'Mind you're here at six o'clock,' were Mr Fitzgibbon's parting words.

She agreed to that happily; she was free for almost six hours and she knew exactly what she was going to go and do. She couldn't expect lunch at Mrs Twist's; she would go and change and have lunch out, take a look at the shops along the Brompton Road and peek into Harrods, take a brisk walk in the park, have tea and get back in good time.

All of which she did, and, much refreshed, presented herself at the consulting-rooms with ten minutes to spare. All the same, he was there before her.

He bade her good evening with his usual cool courtesy and added, 'You will remain with the patient at all times, Miss Napier,' before returning to his writing.

Mrs Keane wasn't there; Florence waited in the reception-room until the bell rang, and opened the door. She wasn't a theatre-goer herself and she had little time for TV; all the same, she recognised the woman who came in. No longer young, but still striking-looking and expertly made-up, exquisitely dressed, delicately perfumed. She pushed past Florence with a nod.

'I hope I'm not to be kept waiting,' she said sharply. 'You'd better let Mr Fitzgibbon know that I'm here.'

Florence looked down her delicate nose. 'I believe that Mr Fitzgibbon is ready for you. If you will sit down for a moment I will let him know that you're here.'

She tapped on the consulting-room door and went in, closing it behind her. 'Your patient is here, sir.'

'Good, bring her in and stay.'

The next half-hour was a difficult one. No one liked to be told that they probably had cancer of a lung, but, with few exceptions, they accepted the news with at least a show of courage. Mr Fitzgibbon, after a lengthy examination, offered his news in the kindest possible way and was answered by a storm of abuse, floods of tears and melodramatic threats of suicide.

Florence kept busy with cups of tea, tissues and soothing words, and cringed at the whining voice going on and on about the patient's public, her ruined health and career, her spoilt looks.

When she at length paused for breath Mr Fitzgibbon said suavely, 'My dear lady, your public need know nothing unless you choose to tell them, and I imagine that you are sufficiently well known for a couple of months away from the stage to do no harm. There is no need to tamper with your looks; your continuing—er—appearance is entirely up to you. Fretting and worrying will do more harm than a dozen operations.'

He waited while Florence soothed a fresh outburst of tears and near-hysterics. 'I suggest that you choose which hospital you prefer as soon as possible and I will operate—within the next three weeks. No later than that.'

'You're sure you can cure me?'

'If it is within my powers to do so, yes.'

'I won't be maimed?'

He looked coldly astonished. 'I do not maim my patients; this is an operation which is undertaken very frequently and gives excellent results.'

'I shall need the greatest care and nursing—I am a very sensitive person...'

'Any of the private hospitals in London will guarantee that. Please let me know when you have made your decision and I will make the necessary arrangements.'

Mr Fitzgibbon got to his feet and bade his patient a polite goodbye, and Florence showed her out.

When she got back he was still sitting at his desk. He took a look at her face and observed, 'I did tell you that it was hard work. At Colbert's I see as many as a dozen a week with the same condition and not one of them utters so much as a whimper.'

'Well,' said Florence, trying to be fair, 'she is famous...'

'Mothers of families are famous too in their own homes, and they face a hazardous future, and what about the middle-aged ladies supporting aged parents, or the women bringing up children on their own?'

Florence so far forgot herself as to sit down on the other side of his desk. 'Well, I didn't know that you were like that...'

'Like what?'

'Minding about people. Oh, doctors and surgeons must mind, I know that, but you...' She paused, at a loss for getting the right words, getting slowly red in the face at the amused mockery on his.

'How fortunate it is, Miss Napier,' he observed gently, 'that my life's happiness does not depend on your good opinion of me.'

She got off the chair. 'I'm sorry, I don't know why I had to say that.' She added ingenuously, 'I often say things without thinking first—Father is always telling me...'

He said carelessly, 'Oh, I shouldn't let it worry you, I don't suppose you ever say anything profound enough to shatter your hearer's finer feelings.'

Florence opened her mouth to answer that back, thought better of it at the last minute, and asked in a wooden voice, 'Do you expect any more patients, sir, or may I tidy up?'

She might not have spoken. 'Do you intend to leave at the end of the month?' he asked idly.

'Leave? Here? No...' She took a sharp breath. 'Do you want me to? I dare say I annoy you. Not everyone can get on with everyone else,' she explained in a reasonable voice, 'you know, a kind of mutual antipathy...'

He remained grave, but his eyes gleamed with amusement. 'I have no wish for you to leave, Miss Napier; you suit me very well: you are quick and sensible and the patients appear to like you, and any grumbling you may do about awkward hours you keep to yourself. We must contrive to rub along together, must we not?' He stood up. 'Now do whatever it is you have to do and we will go somewhere and have a meal.'

Florence eyed him in astonishment. 'You and I? But Mrs Twist will have something keeping warm in the oven for me...'

He reached for the telephone. 'In that case I will ask her to take it out before it becomes inedible.' He waved a large hand at her. 'Fifteen minutes—I've some notes to write up. Come back here when you're ready.'

There seemed no point in arguing with him; Florence sped away to the examination-room and began to put it to rights. Fifteen minutes wasn't long enough, of course;

she would have to see to most of the instruments he had used in the morning—she could come early and do that. She worked fast and efficiently so that under her capable hands the room was pristine once more. The waiting-room needed little done in it; true, on her way out the patient had given vent to her feelings by tossing a few cushions around, but Florence shook them up smartly and repaired to the cloakroom, where she did her face and hair with the speed of light, got out of the uniform and into the jersey dress and matching jacket, thrust her feet into low-heeled pumps, caught up her handbag and went back to the consulting-room.

Mr Fitzgibbon was standing at the window, looking out into the street below, his hands in his pockets. He looked over his shoulder as she went in. 'Do you like living in London?' he wanted to know.

'Well, I don't really live here, do I? I work here, but when I'm free I go home, so I don't really know what living here is like. At Colbert's I went out a good deal when I was off duty, but I never felt as though I belonged.'

'You prefer the country?'

'Oh, yes. Although I should think that if I lived here in surroundings such as these——' she waved an arm towards the street outside '—London might be quite pleasant.'

He opened the door for her and locked it behind him. 'Do you live in London?' she asked.

'Er—for a good deal of the time, yes.' There was a frosty edge to his voice which warned her not to ask questions. She followed him out to the car and was ushered in in silence.

She hadn't travelled in a Rolls-Royce before and she was impressed by its size; it and Mr Fitzgibbon, she reflected, shared the same vast, dignified appearance. She uttered the thought out loud. 'Of course, this is exactly the right car for you, isn't it?'

He was driving smoothly through quiet streets. 'Why?'

'Well, for one thing the size is right, isn't it?' She paused to think. 'And, of course, it has great dignity.'

Mr Fitzgibbon smiled very slightly. 'I am reassured to think that your opinion of me is improving.'

She couldn't think of the right answer to that; instead she asked, 'Where are we going?'

'Wooburn Common, about half an hour from here. You know the Chequers Inn? I've booked a table.'

'Oh—it's in the country?'

'Yes. I felt that it was the least I could do in the face of your preference for rural parts.'

'Well, that's awfully kind of you to take so much trouble. I mean, there are dozens of little cafés around Wimpole Street—well, not actually very near, but down some of the side-streets.'

'I must bear that in mind. Which reminds me, Mrs Twist asks that you should make sure that the cat doesn't get out as you go in.'

'Oh, Buster. She's devoted to him—he's a splendid tabby; not as fine as our Charlie Brown, though. Do you like cats?'

'Yes, we have one; she keeps my own dog company.'

'We have a Labrador—Higgins. He's elderly.' She fell silent, mulling over the way he had said 'we have one', and Mr Fitzgibbon waited patiently for the next question, knowing what it was going to be.

'Are you married?' asked Florence.

'No—why do you ask?'

'Well, if you were I don't think we should be going
out like this without your wife... I expect you think I'm
silly.'

'No, but do I strike you as the kind of man who would
take a girl out while his wife actually sat at home waiting
for him?'

Florence looked sideways at his calm profile. 'No.'

'That, from someone who is still not sure if she likes
me or not, is praise indeed.'

They drove on in silence for a few minutes until she
said in a small resolute voice, 'I'm sorry if I annoyed
you, Mr Fitzgibbon.'

'Contrary to your rather severe opinion of me, I don't
annoy easily. Ah—here we are. I hope you're hungry?'

The Chequers Inn was charming. Florence, ushered
from the car and gently propelled towards it, stopped a
minute to take a deep breath of rural air. It wasn't as
good as Dorset, but it compared very favourably with
Wimpole Street. The restaurant was just as charming,
with a table in a window and a friendly waiter who addressed Mr Fitzgibbon by name and suggested in a quiet
voice that the duck, served with a port wine and pink
peppercorn sauce, was excellent and might please him
and the young lady.

Florence, when consulted, agreed that it sounded delicious, and agreed again when Mr Fitzgibbon suggested
that a lobster mousse with cucumber might be pleasant
to start their meal.

She knew very little about wine, so she took his word
for it that the one poured for her was a pleasant drink,
as indeed it was, compared with the occasional bottle
of table wine which graced the vicarage table. She remarked upon this in the unselfconscious manner that
Mr Fitzgibbon was beginning to enjoy, adding, 'But I

dare say there are a great many wines—if one had the interest in them—to choose from.'

He agreed gravely, merely remarking that the vintage wine he offered her was thought to be very agreeable.

The mousse and duck having been eaten with relish, Florence settled upon glazed fruit tart and cream, and presently poured coffee for them both, making conversation with the well-tried experience of a vicar's daughter, and Mr Fitzgibbon, unexpectedly enjoying himself hugely, encouraged her. It was Florence, glancing at the clock, who exclaimed, 'My goodness, look at the time!' She added guiltily, 'I hope you didn't have any plans for your evening—it's almost ten o'clock.' She went on apologetically, 'It was nice to have someone to talk to.'

'One should, whenever possible, relax after a day's work,' observed Mr Fitzgibbon smoothly.

The nearby church clocks were striking eleven o'clock when he stopped before Mrs Twist's little house. Florence, unfastening her seatbelt, began her thank-you speech, which he ignored while he helped her out, took the key from her, unlocked the door and then stood looming over her.

'I find it quite unnecessary to address you as Miss Napier,' he remarked in the mildest of voices. 'I should like to call you Florence.'

'Well, of course you can.' She smiled widely at him, so carried away by his friendly voice that she was about to ask him what his name was. She caught his steely eye just in time, coughed instead, thanked him once again and took back her key.

He opened the door for her. 'Mind Buster,' he reminded her, and shut the door smartly behind her. She stood leaning against it, listening to the silky purr of the car as he drove away. Buster, thwarted in his attempt to spend the night out, waited until she had started up the narrow stairs and then sidled up behind her, to curl up presently on her bed. Strictly forbidden, but Florence never gave him away.

If she had expected a change in Mr Fitzgibbon's remote manner towards her, Florence was to be disappointed. Despite the fact that he addressed her as Florence, it might just as well have been Miss Napier. She wasn't sure what she had expected, but she felt a vague disappointment, which she dismissed as nonsense in her normal matter-of-fact manner, and made a point of addressing him as 'sir' at every opportunity. Something which Mr Fitzgibbon noted with hidden amusement.

It was very nearly the weekend again, and there were no unexpected hold-ups to prevent her catching the evening train. It was almost the middle of May, and the vicarage, as her father brought the car to a halt before its half-open door, looked welcoming in the twilight. Florence nipped inside and down the wide hall to the kitchen, where her mother was taking something from the Aga.

'Macaroni cheese,' cried Florence happily, twitching her beautiful nose. 'Hello, Mother.' She embraced her parent and then stood her back to look at her. 'You're not doing too much? Is Miss Payne being a help?'

'Yes, dear, she's splendid, and I've never felt better. But how are you?'

'Nicely settled in—the work's quite interesting too, and Mrs Twist is very kind.'

'And Mr Fitzgibbon?'

'Oh, he's a very busy man, Mother. He has a large practice besides the various hospitals he goes to...'

'Do you like him, dear?' Mrs Napier sounded offhand.

'He's a very considerate employer,' said Florence airily. 'Shall I fetch Father? He went round to the garage.'

'Please, love.' Mrs Napier watched Florence as she went, wondering why she hadn't answered her question.

Sunday evening came round again far too soon, but as Florence got into the train at Sherborne she found, rather to her surprise, that she was quite looking forward to the week ahead. Hanging out of the window, saying a last goodbye to her father, she told him this, adding, 'It's so interesting, Father—I see so many people.'

A remark which in due course he relayed to his wife.

'Now, isn't that nice?' observed Mrs Napier. Perhaps by next weekend Florence might have more to say about Mr Fitzgibbon. Her motherly nose had smelt a rat concerning that gentleman, and Florence had barely mentioned him...

Florence, rather unwillingly, had found herself thinking about him. Probably because she still wasn't sure if she liked him, even though he had given her a splendid dinner. She walked round to the consulting-rooms in the sunshine of a glorious May morning, and even London—that part of London, at least—looked delightful. Mrs Keane hadn't arrived yet; Florence got the examination-room ready, opened the windows, put everything out for coffee, filled the kettle for the cup of tea she and Mrs Keane had when there was time, and went to look at the appointment book.

The first patient was to come at nine o'clock—a new patient, she noted, so the appointment would be a long one. The two following were short: old patients for check-ups; she could read up their notes presently. She frowned over the next entry, written in Mrs Keane's hand, for it was merely an address—that of a famous stately home open to the public—and when that lady arrived she asked about it.

Mrs Keane came to peer over her shoulder. 'Oh, yes, dear. A patient Mr Fitzgibbon visits—not able to come here. He'll go straight to Colbert's from there. Let's see, he'll be there all the afternoon, I should think—often goes back there in the evening on a Monday, to check on the operation cases, you know. So there's only Lady Hempdon in the afternoon, and she's not until half-past four.' She hung up her jacket and smoothed her neat old-fashioned hairstyle. 'We've time for tea.'

The first patient arrived punctually, which was unfortunate because there was no sign of Mr Fitzgibbon. Mrs Keane was exchanging good-mornings and remarks about the weather, when the phone rang. Florence went into the consulting-room to answer it.

'Mrs Peake there?' It was to be one of those days; no time lost on small courtesies.

'Yes, just arrived, sir.'

'I shall be ten minutes. Do the usual, will you? And take your time.' Mr Fitzgibbon hung up while she was uttering the 'Yes, sir'.

Mrs Peake was thin and flustered and, under her nice manner, scared. Florence led her to the examination-room, explaining that before Mr Fitzgibbon saw new patients he liked them to be weighed, have their blood-pressure taken and so on. She went on talking in her pleasant voice, pausing to make remarks about this and that as she noted down particulars. More than ten minutes had gone by by the time she had finished, and she was relieved to see the small red light over the door leading to the consulting-room flicker. 'If you will come this way, Mrs Peake—I think I have all the details Mr Fitzgibbon needs from me.'

Mr Fitzgibbon rose from his chair as they went in, giving a distinct impression that he had been sitting there for half an hour or more. His, 'Good morning, Mrs Peake,' was uttered in just the right kind of voice—cheerfully confident—and he received Florence's notes with a courteous, 'Thank you, Sister; be good enough to wait.'

As Florence led Mrs Peake away later she had to admit that Mr Fitzgibbon had a number of sides to him which she had been absolutely unaware of; he had treated his patient with the same cheerfulness, nicely tempered by sympathetic patience, while he wormed, word by word, her symptoms from her. Finally when he had finished he told her very simply what was to be done.

'It's quite simple,' he had reassured her. 'I have studied the X-rays which your doctor sent to me; I can remove a small piece of your lung and you will be quite yourself in a very short time—indeed, you will feel a new woman.' He had gone on to talk about hospitals and convenient dates and escorted her to the door, smiling very kindly at her as he had shaken hands.

Mrs Peake had left, actually smiling. At the door she had pressed Florence's hand. 'What a dear man, my dear, and I trust him utterly.'

There was time to take in his coffee before the next patient arrived. Florence, feeling very well disposed towards him, saw at once that it would be a waste of time. He didn't look up. 'Thank you. Show Mr Cranwell in when he comes; I shan't need you, Sister.'

She wasn't needed for the third patient either, and since after a cautious peep she found the examination-room empty, she set it silently to rights. If Mr Fitzgibbon was in one of his lofty moods then it was a good thing he was leaving after his patient had gone.

She ushered the elderly man out and skipped back smartly to the consulting-room in answer to Mr Fitzgibbon's raised voice.

'I shall want you with me. Five minutes to tidy yourself. I'll be outside in the car.'

She flew to the cloakroom, wondering what she had done, and, while she did her face, set her cap at a more becoming angle and made sure her uniform was spotless, she worried. Had she annoyed a patient or forgotten something? Perhaps he had been crossed in love, unable to take his girlfriend out that evening. They might have quarrelled . . . She would have added to these speculations, only Mrs Keane poked her head round the door.

'He's in the car . . .'

Mr Fitzgibbon leaned across and opened the door as she reached the car, and she got in without speaking, settled herself without looking at him and stared ahead as he drove away.

He negotiated a tangle of traffic in an unflurried manner before he spoke. 'I can hear your thoughts, Florence.'

So she was Florence now, was she? 'In that case,' she said crisply, 'there is no need for me to ask where we are going, sir.'

Mr Fitzgibbon allowed his lip to twitch very slightly. 'No—of course, you will have read about it for yourself. You know the place?'

'I've been there with my brothers.'

'The curator has apartments there; his wife is a patient of mine, recently out of hospital. She is a lady of seventy-two and was unfortunate enough to swallow a sliver of glass during a meal, which perforated her oesophagus. I found it necessary to perform a thoracotomy, from which she is recovering. This should be my final visit, although she will come to the consulting-room later on for regular check-ups.'

'Thank you,' said Florence in a businesslike manner. 'Is there anything else that I need to know?'

'No, other than that she is a nervous little lady, which is why I have to take you with me.'

Florence bit back a remark that she had hardly supposed that it was for the pleasure of her company, and neither of them spoke again until they reached their destination.

This, thought Florence, following Mr Fitzgibbon through a relatively small side-door and up an elegant staircase to the private apartments, was something to tell the boys when she wrote to them. The elderly stooping man who had admitted them stood aside for them to go in, and she stopped looking around her and concentrated on the patient.

A dear little lady, sitting in a chair with her husband beside her. Florence led her to a small bedroom presently, and Mr Fitzgibbon examined her without haste before pronouncing her fit and well, and when Florence led her patient back to the sitting-room he was standing at one of the big windows with the curator, discussing the view.

'You will take some refreshment?' suggested the curator, and Florence hoped that Mr Fitzgibbon would say yes; the curator looked a nice, dignified old man who would tell her more about the house...

Mr Fitzgibbon declined with grave courtesy. 'I must get back to Colbert's,' he explained, 'and Sister must return to the consulting-rooms as soon as possible.'

They made their farewells and went back to the car, and as Mr Fitzgibbon opened the door for her he said, 'I'm already late. I'll take you straight back and drop you off at the door. Lady Hempdon has an appointment for half-past four, has she not?'

She got in, and he got in beside her and drove off. 'Perhaps you would like to drop me off so that I can catch a bus?' asked Florence sweetly.

'How thoughtful of you, Florence, but I think not. We should be back without any delay!'

Mr Fitzgibbon, so often right, was for once wrong.

CHAPTER THREE

MR FITZGIBBON ignored the main road back to the heart of the city. Florence, who wasn't familiar with that part of the metropolis, became quite bewildered by the narrow streets lined with warehouses, most of them derelict, shabby, small brick houses and shops, and here and there newly built blocks of high-rise flats. There was, however, little traffic, and his short cuts would bring him very close to Tower Bridge where, presumably, he intended to cross the river.

She stared out at the derelict wharfs and warehouses they were passing with windows boarded up and walls held upright by wooden props; they looked unsafe and it was a good thing that the terrace of houses on the other side of the street was in a like state. There was nothing on the street save a heavily laden truck ahead of them, loaded with what appeared to be scrap iron. Mr Fitzgibbon .had slowed, since it wasn't possible to pass, so that he was able to stop instantly when the truck suddenly veered across the street and hit the wall of a half-ruined warehouse, bringing it down in a shower of bricks.

Mr Fitzgibbon reached behind for his bag and opened the door. 'Phone the police—this is Rosemary Lane—lock the car, and join me.' He had gone striding up the road towards the still tumbling bricks and metal. There was no sign of the truck.

Florence dialled 999, gave a succinct description of the accident and its whereabouts, and added that at the moment the only people there were herself and a doctor and would they please hurry since whoever had been in the truck was buried under the debris. It took no time at all to take the keys, lock the car and run up the street to where she could see Mr Fitzgibbon, his jacket hanging on a convenient iron railing, clearing away bricks and sheets of metal, iron pipes and the like.

'They're coming,' said Florence, not wasting words.

Mr Fitzgibbon grunted. 'Stand there—I'll pass back to you and you toss it behind you, never mind where. The cabin will be just about here—if I could just get a sight of it...'

He shifted an iron sheet very gently and sent a shower of bricks sliding away so that he was able to pull out a miscellany of bricks and rubble. He passed these back piece by piece to Florence, stopping every now and then to listen.

There was a great deal of dust and they were soon covered in it. A sudden thought made Florence say urgently, 'Oh, do be careful of your hands...' She wished she hadn't said it the moment she had spoken—it had been a silly thing to say. What were cuts and bruises when a man's life was possibly at stake? Only the hands belonged to a skilled surgeon...

Seconds later Mr Fitzgibbon stopped suddenly, and Florence, clasping a nasty piece of concrete with wires sticking out of it, stood, hardly breathing, her ears stretched. Somewhere inside the heap of debris a voice was calling feebly. 'Oi,' it said.

Mr Fitzgibbon passed a couple of bricks to Florence. 'Hello, there!' He sounded cheerful. 'Hang on, we're almost there.'

It took several more minutes before he pulled another lump of concrete clear, exposing part of a man's face, coated with dust, just as an ambulance came to a halt beside them, and hard on its heels a police car and a fire engine.

Mr Fitzgibbon withdrew his head cautiously. 'There's a sheet of metal holding most of the stuff—we need the bricks and rubble out of the way so that we can get at him.'

The newcomers were experts; they widened the gap, shored up the metal above the man's head and brought up their equipment for Mr Fitzgibbon's use. He was head and shoulders inside now; Florence could hear him talking to the man, but he emerged very shortly. 'I need access to his legs. Can you clear the rubble from that end? As far as I can see, he's lying in a tunnel. It seems safe enough above his head, but I need to look at his legs. I believe he's pinned down.' He looked over his shoulder. 'Florence, my bag—I want a syringe and a morphia ampoule.'

He checked the drug and told her to draw it up, and slid into the gap again. The men were already busy, carefully shifting rubble from one end over the man's foot, and presently a boot came into view, and then the other foot, and Mr Fitzgibbon went to have a look.

'I'll have my bag,' he said to Florence. 'Tell the medics I want the amputation kit, then cram yourself through the gap and be ready to do what I tell you.' He spoke to the two men who had come to help him, and she slid carefully towards the man, already drowsy from the morphia.

'Cor, lumme,' he whispered, 'getting the VIP treatment, ain't I? And what's a pretty girl like you doin' 'ere?'

The space was small around the man, and Florence found Mr Fitzgibbon's face within inches of her own.

He was applying a tourniquet above the man's knee. He said easily, 'Oh, Florence is my right hand. Pretty as a picture, isn't she? You ought to see her when her face is clean. Now, old chap, I'm afraid I shall have to take off part of your leg; you won't know anything about it, and I'll promise you'll be as good as new by the time I've finished with you in hospital. Just below the knee, Florence; let go when I say, and keep an eye open for everything else.'

He stretched behind him. 'I'll have that drip—hang on to your end, will you, while I get the needle in?'

He was busy for a few moments, talking quietly to the man as he worked, and when Florence moved a little and something tore he said, 'I hope that's nothing vital, Florence,' and the man chuckled sleepily.

''Old me 'and,' he told Florence, 'and keep an eye on old sawbones...'

Florence gave the grimy fist a squeeze. 'That's a promise.'

Mr Fitzgibbon shifted his bulk very slightly, and another face appeared. A young cheerful face, which winked at Florence. 'Going to put you off to sleep, old chap.'

He had the portable anaesthetic with him, and she said in a comfortable voice, 'And while he's doing it you can tell me about yourself. Are you married? Yes? And children, I expect... Three? I always think that three is a nice number...' She rambled on for a few more moments until the man was unconscious, then she took her hand from his and leaned forward as far as she could, ready to do whatever Mr Fitzgibbon wanted done.

He was working very fast, his gloved hands, despite their size, performing their task with gentleness, cutting and tying and snipping until he said, 'Let go slowly, Florence.'

She loosened the tourniquet very slightly, and then gradually slackened it. Everything held. Mr Fitzgibbon put his hand behind him for the dressings, and his helper had them ready. 'How's his pulse?'

'Strong, fast, regular. You'll take him out from your end?'

'Yes, support his head as far as you can reach.'

He disappeared from her view, but presently he and one of the medics crawled in again and began to shift the man while the third steadied the leg. It took some time; to Florence, her shoulders and arms aching from keeping the man's head and shoulders steady, it seemed like hours. At last he was free, loaded on to a stretcher and taken to the ambulance. She began to wriggle out backwards, and halfway there was caught round the waist and swung on to her feet by Mr Fitzgibbon.

'Stay there,' he told her and went back to talk to the ambulancemen, and she stayed, having no wish to move another step. She ached all over, she was filthy dirty, her mouth was full of dust and she wanted a cup of tea and a hot bath at that very minute; she also wanted to have a good cry, just by way of relieving her feelings.

Her wishes, however, were not to be granted, at least for the moment. Mr Fitzgibbon came back, took her by the arm and walked her to his car. 'In you get; I want to get to Colbert's at the same time as that ambulance.'

He waved to the police car and the fire engine as he came abreast of them, and the police car went ahead, its lights flashing and its siren wailing, and the fire engine brought up the rear.

They went very fast and the traffic parted for them rather like the waters of the Red Sea; at any other time Florence would have enjoyed it immensely.

'Has he got a chance?' she asked.

'Yes. I don't think there's much else damaged, but we can't be sure until he's X-rayed. I want to get at that leg, though—I'll need Fortesque! Ring Colbert's, will you, and see if you can get him?'

Mr Fortesque, the orthopaedic consultant, was found, and yes, he would make himself available, and yes, he'd get Theatre Sister on to it right away. Florence relayed the information as Mr Fitzgibbon drove, and was about to hang up when he said, 'Tell them I want a taxi at the hospital to take you home to Mrs Twist. You're not hurt or cut?'

'No, I don't think so.'

'Make sure of that. Go to Casualty if you have any doubts.' He gave her a brief grin. 'Good, we're here. I'll see you later.' He got out and opened her door. 'Get hold of Mrs Keane. I'll phone later.'

He had gone, but not before giving her an urgent shove towards the taxi waiting for her.

The driver got out and helped her into the cab. 'Been in an accident, love?' he wanted to know. 'Not hurt, are you?'

'No, I'm fine, just very dirty. We stopped to help a man trapped in his truck.' She gave him a shaky smile. 'If you'd take me to my rooms, then I can go back on duty...'

'Right away, love...where to?'

He got out and helped her from the cab, and she said, 'Can you wait a minute? I've not got any money with me but I can get some from my room...'

'All taken care of, love. Head porter at Colbert's told me to call back for it. Just you go in and have a nice cuppa and a lay down.'

He went to the door with her and thumped the knocker and, when Mrs Twist came, handed her over in a fatherly manner. ''Ad an accident,' he told her erroneously. 'I'll leave 'er to your loving 'ands.'

Florence thanked him. 'I'm sure Mrs Twist will give you a cup of tea.'

'Ta, love, but I'd best get back. Take care.'

Mrs Twist shut the door. 'Whatever's happened?' she wanted to know. 'Are you hurt? You're covered in dirt...'

Florence said, 'Not an accident. If you would let me have an old sheet or something I could take these things off here; otherwise the house will get dirty.'

'That's a bit of sense.' Mrs Twist bustled away, arranged an old tablecloth on the spotless lino in the hall, and begged Florence to stand on it. She peeled off everything, with Mrs Twist helping. 'And this dress is ruined,' declared that lady. 'There's a great piece torn out of the back; lucky there wasn't anyone to see your knickers.'

Mr Fitzgibbon must have had a splendid view when he had lifted her out of the truck. 'If I could have a bath and wash my hair, Mrs Twist?'

'That you may, love, and a nice hot cup of tea first. And how about a nice nap in bed?'

'I haven't the time. Mr Fitzgibbon has a patient at half-past four; I must get back to get ready for her.'

'You've not had your dinner?'

'No.'

'I'll have a sandwich or two for you when you've had your bath. Now off you go.'

Later, her head swathed in a towel, comfortable in a dressing-gown and slippers, Florence sat in Mrs Twist's kitchen, gobbling sandwiches and drinking endless cups of tea while she told her landlady all about it. Halfway through she remembered that she had to phone Mrs Keane and, since it was an emergency and Mrs Twist found the whole thing exciting, she was allowed to use the phone. Mrs Keane reacted with calm. 'You come over when you're ready,' she told Florence. 'We'll have a cup of tea, and by then I could ring Colbert's and see if Mr Fitzgibbon has any instructions for us. You're sure you're all right?'

'I'm fine.' Florence put down the phone and, urged by Mrs Twist, went on with her account of the morning's events.

There was more tea waiting for her when she got to the consulting-rooms, and Mrs Keane, despite her discreet manner, was avid to hear the details.

'What I don't understand,' said Florence, 'is why Mr Fitzgibbon was going to operate on the patient—he's a chest man...'

'Yes, dear; he specialises in chest surgery, but he can turn his hand to anything, and this Mr Fortesque is an old friend and colleague. Mr Fitzgibbon is a man who, once having started something, likes to see it through to the end.' She passed the biscuit tin. 'And you, dear, were you hurt at all?'

'No, but my uniform is ruined and I caught the back of the skirt on a nail or something and tore a great rent in it. Mrs Twist said she could see my knickers, which means everyone else saw them too.'

'Knickers?' asked Mrs Keane. 'I didn't think girls wore them any more—only those brief things with lace.'

'Well, yes, but I didn't tell Mrs Twist that—she was horrified enough.'

'Probably no one noticed.'

'Mr Fitzgibbon lifted me down from the truck; I was coming out backwards.'

'Mr Fitzgibbon is a gentleman,' declared her companion. 'Have another cup of tea! We have twenty minutes or so still.'

Florence was arranging the surgical impedimenta Mr Fitzgibbon might need when he came into the consulting-room and thrust wide the half-open door connecting the examination-room. If Florence had hoped for a slightly warmer relationship after their morning's experience she saw at once that she was going to be disappointed. He looked exactly as he always did, immaculate, his linen spotless, not a hair out of place, his manner coolly impersonal.

'Ah, Sister, none the worse for your experience, I hope? You feel able to finish the day's work?'

'Yes. What about that poor man? Did he have any other injuries?'

'Fractured ribs, a perforated lung and a fractured humerus. We've patched him up and he should do. He had plenty of pluck.'

'His wife...?'

'She's with him. She'll stay in the hospital for tonight at least.'

'The children?' Florence went on doggedly.

'With Granny.'

'Oh, good. Someone must have organised everything splendidly.'

'Indeed, yes,' agreed Mr Fitzgibbon, who had done the organising, getting this and that done, throwing his weight around rather, and no one daring to gainsay him. Not that he had been other than his usual cool, courteous self.

'Be good enough to give Mrs Keane details of your ruined uniform so that you can be reimbursed, and—er—for any other garment which may have suffered.'

Florence blushed.

No further reference was made to the morning's happenings, and she went off to her room feeling slightly ill done by. Mr Fitzgibbon could have thanked her, or at least expressed concern as to her feelings—did he consider her to be made of stone? Florence, very much a warm-hearted girl, reflected that there must be something wrong with his life, something which made him uncaring of those people around him. But that wasn't true, she had to remind herself; he had been marvellous with the man in the truck—indeed, he had sounded quite different talking to him. Getting ready for bed, she decided that she was sorry for him; he needed someone or something to shake his unshakeable calm. Underneath that he was probably quite nice to know. Her eyes closed on the praiseworthy resolve to treat him with understanding, not to answer back and to show sympathy if he ever showed signs of needing it.

Full of good resolutions, she went to work the next morning, but there was little opportunity of carrying any of them out. Mr Fitzgibbon was decidedly abrupt in his manner towards her, and in the face of that it was hard to remain meek and sympathetic. Nevertheless, she fetched his coffee and bade him drink it in a motherly fashion, pointed out that it was a lovely morning and suggested that a weekend in the country would do him a world of good, adding that he probably didn't take enough exercise.

He raked her with cold eyes. 'Your solicitude for my health flatters me, Florence, but pray confine your concern to the patients.'

So much for her good intentions.

It was towards the end of the week as she was tidying up after a patient that Mrs Keane came in. 'There's Miss Paton here, Mr Fitzgibbon, wants to see you.' She hesitated. 'I did say that you were about to leave for the hospital.'

He looked up from his desk. 'Ask her to come in, will you, Mrs Keane?' He looked across to the half-open door of the examination-room, where Florence was putting away instruments. 'I shan't need you, Florence; if you haven't finished there perhaps you will come back presently?'

He spoke pleasantly but without warmth. She closed the door and crossed the consulting-room, and reached the door just as it was opened from the other side. Out of the corner of her eye she saw Mr Fitzgibbon get to his feet as a girl came in. Not a girl, she corrected herself, taking in the details with a swift feminine eye, but a woman of thirty, good-looking, delicately made-up, dressed with expensive simplicity. She went past Florence with barely a glance.

'Darling, I simply have to see you. Naughty me, coming to your rooms, but you weren't at the party and I have so much...'

Florence reluctantly closed the door on the rather high-pitched voice, but not before she had heard Mr Fitzgibbon's, 'My dear Eleanor, this is delightful...'

'Who's she?' asked Florence, and Mrs Keane for once looked put out.

'Well, I can't say for certain, dear. She seems to be very friendly with Mr Fitzgibbon—she's always phoning him, you know, and sometimes he rings her. She's a widow; married an old man. He died a year or so ago. Very smart, she is—goes everywhere.'

'And does she ... does he ... ? Are they going to get married?'

'If she gets her way they will, but you can't tell with him, dear. Never shows his feelings. Very popular he is, lots of friends, could go anywhere he chooses, but you never know what he's thinking, if you know what I mean.'

Florence thought she knew. 'But she's all wrong for him,' she said urgently.

Mrs Keane nodded, 'Yes, dear, he needs someone who doesn't butter him up—someone like you.'

'Me?' Florence said and laughed. 'Are you going home? I'll have to stay and finish the examination-room. I hope they won't be too long. I said I'd be at Colbert's at seven o'clock.'

'Of course, you've got friends there, I expect. I'll be off. The first patient is at nine o'clock tomorrow—a new one, too.'

After Mrs Keane had gone Florence went and sat in the kitchen, and it was another ten minutes before Mr Fitzgibbon and his visitor came out. She came out to meet him and asked if she should lock up, and then bade them goodnight. 'Who's that girl?' she heard Eleanor ask as they left the waiting-room. She wondered what he had replied, then shrugged her shoulders, finished her work and went home in her turn.

She had her supper on a tray in her room, changed quickly and went to catch a bus to Colbert's. The man who had been in the truck was out of Intensive Care and, since she had been on the hospital staff, she had no difficulty in obtaining permission to visit him.

She found him propped up in bed, looking very much the worse for wear but cheerfully determined to get better. His wife was with him; a small, thin woman whose nondescript appearance Florence guessed held as determined a nature as his. She didn't stay long; she arranged the flowers she had brought with her in a vase, expressed her delight at seeing him already on the road to recovery, and prepared to leave.

'Owes 'is life to you and that nice doctor,' said his wife as Florence prepared to say goodbye. 'Bless yer both for saving 'im. And that doctor. 'E's a gent if ever there was one. 'Aving me fetched like 'e did, and all fixed up to stay as long as I want, and the kids seen to. Not to mention the money. A loan, of course; as soon as we can we'll pay 'im back, but there's no denying the cash'll come in handy.'

Going back to her bedsit, Florence reflected that Mr Fitzgibbon was a closed book as far as she was concerned. And likely to remain so.

The next day was Friday and she would be going home in the evening. The day was much as any other; Mr Fitzgibbon never lacked for patients—his appointments book was filled weeks ahead and a good deal of each day was spent at the hospital. Florence cleared up after the last patient that afternoon, glad to be going home. Mr Fitzgibbon had been his usual terse self, and she felt the strong need for the carefree atmosphere of the vicarage.

She tidied away the last dressing towels, wiped the glass top of the small table to a brilliant shine and opened the door into the waiting-room. Mr Fitzgibbon was sitting on the corner of Mrs Keane's desk, talking to her, but he turned to look at Florence and got to his feet.

'I have just agreed to see a patient this evening, Florence. He is unable to come at any other time so we must alter our plans. You were going home this evening?'

She wouldn't have minded so much if she had thought he had sounded even slightly sympathetic. 'Yes, but there are plenty of morning trains—I can go tomorrow. At what time this evening do you want me here, sir?'

'Half-past six. Telephone your home now, if you wish.'

He nodded and smiled at Mrs Keane, and then went away.

'Hard luck, dear,' said Mrs Keane. 'Is there a later train you could catch?'

'It takes two hours to get to Sherborne and it would be too late for anyone to fetch me. No, it's all right, I'll go on the early train in the morning.'

'Is Mrs Twist home? What about your supper?'

'She's going out, but that's all right, I can open a tin of beans or something. I told her I'd be going home, you see.'

'It's spoilt Mr Fitzgibbon's evening too—he was to have taken someone out to dinner. I dare say it's that woman who came here—that Eleanor...'

'Well, it's nice to know that his evening is spoilt too,' said Florence waspishly. She smiled suddenly. 'And hers.'

Mrs Keane laughed. 'I'll be off; you're coming?'

They went out together, and Mrs Keane said cheerfully, 'See you Monday. He's operating at eight o'clock, so we'll have the morning to ourselves.'

Mrs Twist was put out. 'If I'd known I'd have got you a bit of ham for your supper...'

Florence hastened to placate her. 'If I may open a tin of beans? I'll do some toast. I've no idea how long it's going to take; Mr Fitzgibbon didn't say. I'll catch the early train tomorrow morning...'

'Well, if that's all right with you,' said Mrs Twist reluctantly. 'Just this once. Seeing it's for Mr Fitzgibbon.'

Florence let that pass. She doubted if he would need to open a tin of beans for his supper. She had her tea, tidied her already tidy person, took a quick look at Mrs Twist's *Daily Mirror* and went back to the consulting-room.

Mr Fitzgibbon was already there, brooding over some X-rays. 'Ah, there you are,' he observed, for all the world as though she were late instead of being five minutes early. He went back to his contemplation of the films and she took herself off to the waiting-room, ready to admit the patient.

He arrived fifteen minutes late, and Florence opened the door to him, recognising the famous features so often pictured on the front pages of the daily Press and the evening news on TV. She hoped that her face betrayed no surprise as she wished him good evening and begged him to take a seat. 'Mr Fitzgibbon is here,' she said, 'if you'll wait a moment.'

It struck her much later that one didn't ask men like that to wait a moment, but Mr Fitzgibbon had at that moment thrust open his door and come to shake hands with his patient. He nodded to Florence and she followed them into the consulting-room to hear him assure the man that she was utterly reliable and discreet. 'Sister will prepare the examination-room while I check the details your doctor has given me,' suggested Mr Fitzgibbon smoothly, and Florence, taking the hint, slid away and closed the door.

It seemed a long time before the two men came to the examination-room, and an even lengthier time before Mr Fitzgibbon was finished with his examination. The pair of them went back into the consulting-room, leaving

Florence to clear up. Mr Fitzgibbon appeared to have used almost everything usable there—an hour's work at least, she thought, and it was already almost eight o'clock.

She was half finished when he came in. His patient had gone and there was only the reading-lamp on his desk to light the consulting-room.

He said pleasantly, 'I'm sorry that your evening has been spoilt.' He picked up a hand towel from the pile she had just arranged. 'Mrs Twist has supper waiting for you?'

'Oh, yes,' said Florence airily, 'something special.' She said, 'She's a good cook, and I expect we shall have it together...'

Mr Fitzgibbon replaced the towel carefully. 'In that case, there's no point in suggesting that we might have had a meal somewhere together.'

'Was your evening spoilt too?' asked Florence, aware that it had been, but hoping for a few details.

'Spoilt? Hardly. Shall I say that it necessitated a change of plans?'

'Me too,' agreed Florence with a cheerful lack of grammar. 'Never mind, you have the whole weekend.'

'Indeed I have. Be outside Mrs Twist's at half-past eight tomorrow morning, Florence: I will drive you home.'

She arranged everything just so, put the hand towels out of his reach and finally said, 'That is most kind of you, sir, but there is a train I can catch... It only takes two hours; I can be home well before lunchtime.'

'Two hours? I can do it in an hour and a half in the car. I need a breath of country air too.'

'Won't it spoil your day?' asked Florence feebly.

'My dear Florence, if it were going to spoil my day I should not have suggested it in the first place.'

She looked extremely pretty standing there, the last of the sun turning her hair to burnished copper, her face a little tired, for it had been a long day. She gave him a clear look, making sure that he had meant what he had said. 'Then I'd like that very much,' she told him quietly.

'Go home now, Florence. I have some writing to do, so I'll lock up.' He turned back to his desk. 'Goodnight.'

She wished him a good night and made her way to Mrs Twist's, where she kicked off her shoes, opened a tin of baked beans, took the pins out of her hair and sat on the kitchen table, eating her supper. Of course, supper with Mr Fitzgibbon would have been quite a different matter—a well-chosen meal at the end of the day would have been very acceptable, but not acting as a substitute for the glamorous Eleanor.

She fed Buster, had a bath and presently went to bed.

It was a glorious morning; it was almost June and a lovely time of the year. She swapped the dress she had been going to wear for a much prettier one, telling herself it was because it was more suited to the bright sunshine outside, and she skipped downstairs to make a cup of tea. Mrs Twist took things easy on Saturdays and there would be no breakfast, although Florence knew she was free to help herself. The note she had left on the kitchen table for her landlady had gone, and in its place Mrs Twist had left one of her own. 'Don't let Buster out. Have a nice trip, you lucky girl.'

Florence drank her tea, gave Buster his breakfast, picked up her weekend bag and let herself out of the house. She was closing the door gently behind her when the Rolls came to quite a quiet halt and Mr Fitzgibbon got out to open her door.

She wished him good morning and thought how nice he looked in casual clothes; he looked younger too, and his 'good morning' was uttered in a friendly voice. Emboldened, she remarked upon the beauty of the morning, but beyond a brief reply he had nothing to say and she supposed that he wasn't in the mood for conversation. She let out a small surprised yelp when a warm tongue gently licked the back of her neck. She turned her head and found herself looking into a pair of gentle brown eyes in a whiskered face, heavily shrouded in eyebrows and a great deal of light brown hair.

'Ah, I should have mentioned,' said Mr Fitzgibbon casually, 'Monty likes the country too. You don't mind?'

'Mind? No, of course not. She has a beautiful face. What is she?'

'We have often wondered... We settled for a mixed parentage.'

'Did you get her from a breeder or a pet shop?'

'Neither—from a doorway in a street full of boarded-up houses. It took some time for her to achieve the physical perfection she now enjoys, but, even now, it is difficult to decide what her parents might be.'

Florence exchanged another look with the brown eyes behind her. 'She's awfully sweet. Higgins will love her. I'm not sure about Charlie Brown, though—he's our cat.'

'Monty likes cats. Our cat had kittens a couple of weeks ago and she broods over the whole basketful whenever Melisande goes walking.'

'Melisande—the cat?'

'Yes. Does your mother know that we're coming?'

'Yes. My brothers are home again for half-term.'

They lapsed into silence again, broken only by Monty's gentle sighs and mutterings. They were on the A303 by now and the road was fairly clear, for it was still early. Florence, sitting back in the comfortable seat with the dog's warm breath on her neck, felt happy and, since there seemed to be no need to talk, she took time to wonder why. Of course, being driven in a Rolls-Royce was enough to make anyone happy, but it was more than that: she was enjoying Mr Fitzgibbon's company, even though he was doing nothing at all to entertain her. She felt quite at ease with him, and the thought surprised her, for until that moment she had got used to the idea that she didn't much like him, only, she had to admit, sometimes.

Presently she ventured to remark that he could turn off at Sparkford, and then added, 'Oh, sorry, you came with Mr Wilkins.' Then, because he didn't answer, 'Do you like this part of England?'

'Very much; an easy drive from town and, once one is away from the main road, charmingly rural.' He turned off the A303 and took a minor road towards Sherborne, and presently left it for a narrow country road, its hedges burgeoning with the foliage of oncoming summer.

Gussage Tollard lay in a hollow; they could see the house-tops as they went down the hill, and Florence gave a contented sigh. 'Oh, it is nice to be home,' she said.

'You regret taking the job?' Mr Fitzgibbon wanted to know sharply. 'You do not like working for me?'

'Of course I like working for you, it's a super job. Only I wish I knew you better...' She stopped, very red in the face. 'I'm sorry, I don't know what made me say that.'

'Well, if you ever find out, let me know.' He didn't look at her, for which she was thankful. 'The vicarage

is past the church and along the lane, isn't it?' He
sounded so casual that she hoped he might not have
heard what she had said, but he must have done because
he had told her to tell him ... It had been a silly remark
and easily forgotten.

She said cheerfully, 'Here we are.' She glanced at her
watch. 'It took an hour and twenty-five minutes. You
were right.'

'Of course I was.' He spoke without conceit as he got
out, opened her door and then let Monty out, giving her
the chance to run into the house first.

CHAPTER FOUR

FLORENCE hadn't reached the door before her mother came to meet her, and hard on her heels were her two brothers, with Higgins shoving his way past them to jump up at her, barking his pleasure.

Florence said breathlessly, 'Hello, Mother—boys...here's Mr Fitzgibbon.'

He had followed more slowly, and stood quietly with Monty beside him as they all surged towards him.

'You've met each other,' said Florence to her mother, and added, 'these are my brothers—Tom and Nicky. Oh, and this is Higgins...'

Higgins had sat down deliberately in front of Monty, and presently bent his elderly head to breathe gently over the little dog.

'Oh, good, they're going to be friends,' said Mrs Napier. 'Come in—the coffee is ready. Did you have a decent drive from London?'

She led the way indoors, and Mr Fitzgibbon, at his most urbane, gave all the right answers and, when asked, declared that there was nothing he enjoyed more than coffee in the kitchen.

'You see, I'm getting lunch and we can all talk there while I'm cooking.' Mrs Napier gave him a sweet smile. 'Sit here,' she told him, offering a Windsor chair by the big scrubbed table. 'I'm afraid we use the kitchen a great deal, especially in the winter. This is a nice old house but it is all open fireplaces—there's no heating otherwise, and we spend hours lugging in coals just to keep the

sitting-room fire glowing. Thank heaven for an Aga.'
She beamed at him. 'Have you one in your home?'

Mr Fitzgibbon hesitated for a moment. 'Er—yes, I
believe we have.'

'Well, I'm sure you must need it, leading the kind of
life you do... at everybody's beck and call, I dare say.'

She was pouring coffee as she spoke, and Florence
picked up a jug of hot milk. 'Black or white?' she asked
him. She had been listening to her mother rambling on
in her gentle way and not minding in the least; if he
didn't like it it was just too bad.

Apparently he didn't mind; he accepted milk and sugar
and a large slice of the cake on the table, and entered
into a spirited conversation with her brothers concerning cars, although he interlarded this with small talk
with her mother, and presently, when she remarked that
the vicar had gone to Whitehorse Farm a mile the other
side of the village, he suggested he might take the car
and give him a lift back. An idea which appealed to the
boys and which Mrs Napier instantly accepted. 'Do leave
your little dog here if you like; she seems happy enough
with Higgins...'

They all went out to the car again, and when Mr
Fitzgibbon opened the car doors both dogs got in as
well. Florence stood with her mother, watching the car
turn smoothly out of the gate, and her mother said, 'I
do hope he doesn't mind taking the boys and Higgins;
he seems such a nice man—charming manners too. Very
considerate to work for, I've no doubt, love.'

'I suppose so, Mother. Nothing is allowed to stand in
the way of his work, though, and he's very reserved. He
doesn't talk much, only to tell me what he wants done...'

'But, darling, you're not working all the time; you had a two hours' drive from London—you must have talked...?'

Florence cast thoughts back to the morning's journey. 'Well, no, only this and that, you know.'

'I'm surprised that he isn't married,' observed Mrs Napier chattily.

They were in the kitchen, clearing up the coffee-cups. 'I honestly don't think he's had the time to fall in love, although he must know any number of suitable women...'

'Suitable?'

'Well, you know what I mean, Mother. His kind of female, beautifully dressed and made-up and entertaining and witty and not needing to work...'

Mrs Napier gave a mug an extra polish. 'What makes you think that is his kind of female?'

'A girl—no, a woman came to the consulting-rooms, Eleanor something or other, and he seemed awfully pleased to see her. She had one of those voices you actually hear from yards away even though they're not speaking loudly—you know what I mean?'

'I don't know Mr Fitzgibbon well, but he strikes me as a man who is unlikely to succumb to such a woman. Do you suppose he might stay for lunch?'

'I doubt it,' said Florence. 'Here they are now.'

Her father was the only one to come into the kitchen; the others were outside, and Florence could see two youthful heads on either side of a grizzled one, peering into the Rolls's engine.

Her father kissed her and patted her on the shoulder in a paternal fashion.

'My dear, what a very pleasant man your doctor is...'

'He's a surgeon, Father, and he's not mine...'

'No, no, my dear, I speak lightly. So kind of him to drive over to fetch me, and he's so patient with the boys.' He looked at his wife. 'Might he not be invited to lunch?'

'Of course, it's Saturday—he must be free. I'll ask him.'

Presently, back in the kitchen, he refused. 'There is nothing I would have enjoyed more,' he assured Mrs Napier, 'but I have a date this afternoon, added to which I must get back to town.'

'Well, of course you must,' declared Mrs Napier comfortably. 'I don't suppose you have much time in which to enjoy yourself. It was very kind of you to drive Florence here. It's not like her to miss the train.'

'Ah, but that's why I brought her—she didn't miss the train, she had to stay on Friday evening to attend a patient; I sometimes have consultations at awkward hours.'

Mrs Napier, who had been nurturing the beginnings of a possible romance between this nice man and her daughter, was disappointed.

They went to the door to see him off, and Mrs Napier said wistfully, 'A pity you couldn't stay; I would so enjoy hearing about your work—I really am quite vague as to what exactly Florence does...'

He was getting into the car. 'Works very hard, Mrs Napier; she is also clear-headed and brave, and doesn't make a fuss when her clothes get torn and she gets covered in dust.' He turned to grin at Florence's annoyed face. 'Do ask her about it.'

He waved a hand, and drove away with the minimum of fuss.

'What exactly did he mean?' asked Mrs Napier. 'Come indoors, love, and tell us about it. Have you been in an accident?'

'No,' said Florence crossly, 'and I wasn't going to say anything about it. How tiresome he is.'

'Yes, dear. Now sit down and tell us what happened.'

There was nothing for it but to do as her mother asked. 'Really, I didn't do anything; I mean, only what anyone else would have done. It was Mr Fitzgibbon who rescued the man and amputated his leg. He did it on his hands and knees and it must have been very uncomfortable for him as he's so very large. He went straight to Colbert's and there was further surgery to do. He sent me back to my bedsit in a taxi.'

'How very kind.'

'Yes? He expected me to be on duty at the consulting-rooms later that afternoon.' Florence gave an indignant snort. 'He doesn't spare himself, and he doesn't spare anyone else either.'

'He did bring you home in that Rolls,' Tom pointed out. 'I think he's absolutely super...'

'So do I,' said Nicky. 'He knows a lot about cars too.'

'Pooh,' said Florence, 'who wants to know about cars anyway?' And she flounced out of the room and up to her bedroom, where she hung out of the window and brooded, although she wasn't sure what she was brooding about.

It was impossible to brood for long. The garden below her window was bursting with a mixture of early-summer flowers: roses, entangled with soldiers and sailors, wall-flowers, forget-me-nots, pansies, lilies of the valley and buttercups rioted all over the rather neglected flow-erbeds of the vicarage garden. Florence took herself off downstairs, firmly resolved to bring a little order to the colourful chaos.

The weekend was over far too quickly; she left the half-weeded garden with reluctance, aware that the hard work she had put into it had done much to assuage the feeling of restlessness. Sitting in the train on the way back to London, she reflected that a week's hard work would get her back to her normal acceptance of life once more.

Her room looked cramped and dreary after the comfortable shabbiness of the vicarage; she arranged the flowers she had brought back with her, unpacked her overnight bag and took a bunch of roses down to the kitchen for Mrs Twist, who was so delighted with them that she opened a tin of soup to add to their supper of corned beef, lettuce and tomatoes.

She walked to work the next morning, the early sunshine already warm. It was going to be a lovely day, and her thoughts turned longingly to the garden at home and all those roses needing her attention. Once at the consulting-rooms and in Mrs Keane's company, she became her usual self. With Mr Fitzgibbon at the hospital, there was the opportunity to give the examination-room a good clean, check the instruments, see that the cupboards and the drawers were stocked, and have a leisurely cup of coffee with Mrs Keane.

'You got home, then?' asked that lady as they drank it.

'Mr Fitzgibbon gave me a lift on Saturday morning.'

'Well, I never did—how very kind of him. Was he spending the weekend in your part of the world, I wonder?'

'Oh, no. He only stayed for a cup of coffee; he said he had a date...'

'That Eleanor woman, I have no doubt. There were two calls from her on the answering machine. Well, he's not likely to take her out this evening—he won't get away from Colbert's much before one o'clock, and there are five appointments starting at two o'clock.'

Mrs Keane took another biscuit. 'He'll be a bit terse, I dare say. Monday morning and all that.' She asked abruptly, 'Are you going to stay? I do hope so.'

'Heavens, the month is almost up, isn't it? Yes, I hope he'll decide to keep me on. The work's interesting, isn't it? And it's nice being able to go home each weekend. And the money, of course...'

'Well, I don't expect you'll get home every weekend. There's an appointment for Wednesday—a query. In the Midlands. You'll probably have to go with him, perhaps stay overnight; it could easily have been the weekend, even though it isn't this time.'

'Well, that's all right.'

'Good. Do you mind if I go out for half an hour? I must get something for supper tonight and we'll probably be too late for the shops this afternoon.'

Left to herself, Florence did some more turning out of cupboards and drawers, and she answered the phone several times and then turned on the answering machine and listened to Eleanor's voice. She sounded snappy; Mr Fitzgibbon hadn't turned up to take her to the theatre, nor had he bothered to let her know why. The second message was even snappier. Florence, while conceding that Mr Fitzgibbon wasn't a man who needed sympathy, being well able to look after himself, felt quite sorry for him.

Mrs Keane was back, and they had eaten their lunch when he came in. His 'good afternoon' was austere, and he looked tired, which wasn't surprising, since he had been operating since eight o'clock, but as Florence ushered in the first of the patients she saw that he had somehow shed his weariness, presenting to his patients a sympathetic calm and a complete concentration.

The last one went just before five o'clock, and she took in a cup of tea Mrs Keane had ready for him.

He glanced up as she went in. 'I'm going back to Colbert's,' he told her. 'My first appointment is for nine o'clock tomorrow morning, isn't it? If I'm late say all the usual, will you? I'll hope to get here, but I can't be certain.'

She murmured and went to the door, to be halted by his, 'By the way, I have to go to Lichfield on Wednesday—a little girl with cystic fibrosis. She's been a patient of mine for some time, but her parents insisted on taking her home... She's a difficult child and I shall want you with me. It is possible that we shall have to spend the night, so bring a bag with you. We shall leave around midday after the morning appointments. I've engaged to meet her local doctor at half-past two.'

'Uniform, sir?'

'Oh, decidedly, and your starchiest manner. The poor child is spoilt by her parents and an old nanny, but she responds quite well to calm authority.'

Florence said, 'Yes, sir,' and took herself out of the room. A couple of days away from the consulting-rooms would be a nice change, but it sounded as though she was going to have her work cut out. She found Mrs Keane in the kitchen, drinking tea, and she poured herself a cup.

'I'm to go to Lichfield,' she explained, 'and probably stay the night there, as you thought.'

'Oh, Phoebe Villiers—Sister Brice dreaded that visit; the child's very difficult and the parents absolutely refuse to let her have further treatment in hospital. They had a house somewhere in Hampstead, and that's how Mr

Fitzgibbon took her on as a patient; got her into Colbert's and there really was an improvement, but the parents moved to their other house at Lichfield and discharged her. He could have refused to go on treating her as a patient, but he would never do that, not while there was a chance of keeping the child as fit as possible.'

'So he goes all the way up there to see her?'

'Yes, every three months—she's a private patient, of course, but even if she weren't I believe that he would still go. He doesn't give up easily.'

The next day went smoothly enough; it was just as Mr Fitzgibbon was leaving in the evening after a long afternoon that Florence asked, 'Do I have time to go back to Mrs Twist's tomorrow and fetch my overnight bag?'

'I think not. I want to get away in good time. We shall have to stop for a meal of sorts on the way; you can do whatever you do to your face and hair then.'

Florence muttered a reply. The man needed a wife so that he might have some insight into female ways. She wondered if he treated Eleanor in such an arbitrary fashion, and how she responded if he did. Of course, the occasion would never arise; Eleanor had all the time in the world to make herself ready for any social outing, and this, Florence reminded herself briskly, was by no means to be a social visit—not one of them was likely to notice if her hair was all anyhow and her nose shining.

All the same, she washed her hair that evening, attended to her nicely kept hands and packed an extra uniform. She had dealt with difficult children in hospital and knew how prone they were to throw things...

It wanted ten minutes to noon as Mr Fitzgibbon eased the Rolls away from the kerb. Florence, sitting silently beside him, thought of the small tasks she hadn't had time to do, made a mental inventory of the contents of her overnight bag, and tried not to think about lunch. Her breakfast had been a sketchy one that morning and there had been no time for coffee. She hoped her insides wouldn't rumble. Anyone else, she reflected, and she wouldn't have hesitated to say that she was hungry, but a quick peep at her companion's severe profile made it obvious that he wasn't concerned about food. Getting out of London was uppermost in his mind.

Not knowing that part of the city well, she became quite bewildered with the short cuts and the ins and outs of nondescript streets, and once or twice she wondered if he had got lost, but suddenly they were on the M1, going north, and his well-shod foot went down on the accelerator.

'You're a girl after my own heart,' he said, 'you know when to hold your tongue.' After which astonishing remark he lapsed into silence once more, leaving her to wonder whether he had meant that as a compliment or merely an expression of relief; either way it seemed a good idea to stay silent.

The miles flew by, and they had passed the outskirts of Luton when he slowed the car and turned into Toddington Service Station.

'Twenty minutes and not a minute more. Out you get.'

She got out and followed him into the vast and busy cafeteria. 'Coffee and sandwiches?' he asked as he sat her down at a table. 'Any preference?'

'Cheese, and tea, not coffee.' She added after his retreating back, 'Please.'

The place wasn't too full; he was back quickly with his tray: sandwiches for both of them, coffee for him and a little pot of tea for her—she liked him for that.

They didn't waste time talking, but she liked him even better when he said, 'This is hardly the kind of place to which I would take you, Florence, but we are rather pressed for time. You must allow me to give you dinner one evening as recompense.'

She paused before taking another bite. 'That's all right, sir. These sandwiches are very good, and the tea is heavenly.'

She swallowed a second cup and stood up when he asked her if she was ready.

'I'll meet you at the car—I'll be very quick.' She had whisked herself away, not seeing his quick smile at the unselfconscious remark. The image of Eleanor crossed his mind; in like circumstances she would have talked prettily about powdering her nose and kept him waiting for ten minutes. Of course, she would never allow herself to be in surroundings such as these in the first place.

He was back in the car by now and watched Florence emerge from the Ladies' and make a swift beeline towards him.

He opened the door, shut her in once more and got in beside her. The motorway wasn't busy, since it was the lunch-hour, and the Rolls, kept at a steady pace of seventy miles an hour, made light of the distance. Florence, busy with pleasant plans as to the laying out of her first pay cheque, due the next day, was surprised to see the sign to Lichfield ahead of them. Mr Fitzgibbon turned off the motorway. 'Around twelve miles,' he remarked. He glanced at his watch. 'You will probably have five minutes or so before you meet Phoebe.' He glanced at her. 'You look remarkably neat and tidy.'

'I should hope so,' said Florence tartly. 'You wouldn't employ me for long if I weren't.'

'True. Which reminds me—you intend to stay on?'

'Well, yes, if you're quite satisfied with me, sir.'

'Given time, I see no reason why we shouldn't deal excellently with each other.'

The kind of quelling remark which was enough to tempt a girl to give in her notice then and there.

The Villiers lived a few miles from the town, and Florence glanced around as they drove through the double gates and along a driveway as smooth as silk, running through gardens so well laid out that it might have been painted instead of planted. A far cry from the vicarage garden, always in need of a good weed and the pruning shears, and twice as beautiful. The house matched the garden: with its pristine white walls, sparkling windows and glossy paint, it seemed rather like a stage setting. Mr Fitzgibbon, apparently oblivious to his surroundings, got out, opened her door and walked with her to the wide porch.

Florence, still feeling as though she were on a film set, was ushered into the hall by a maid, very correctly dressed, even to a cap on her head, and stood quietly waiting for whatever would happen next.

'Mr Fitzgibbon and Sister Napier—we are expected,' said Mr Fitzgibbon, and she walked beside him as they were shown into a large room with a lofty ceiling and french windows opening on to the garden, and furnished with modern chairs, deep couches and glass-topped tables. Florence, brought up among well-polished oak and mahogany pieces, winced.

The man and woman who came to meet them matched the room. Well-dressed, the woman beautifully made-up and coiffeured, they were as modern as their surroundings.

Mrs Villiers spoke first. 'Mr Fitzgibbon—so good of you to come. Dr Gibbs will be joining us shortly.' Her eyes swept over Florence. 'A new nurse? What happened to the other one?'

'Sister Brice left me to get married—may I introduce Sister Napier, Mrs Villiers?'

Mrs Villiers nodded in Florence's direction without looking at her. 'Well, do sit down and have a drink... Nurse can go to her room for a moment or two.'

'I should prefer her to meet Phoebe before we examine her.' Mr Fitzgibbon's courteous manner was very cool.

'Oh, if she must. The child's with Nanny. I'll get someone to take her up.'

'I think it might be better if I go too. Perhaps I might be told when Dr Gibbs arrives?'

Mrs Villiers laughed and shrugged her shoulders. 'You must do what you think best, I suppose.' She glanced at her silent husband. 'Archie, ring the bell, will you?'

They were led upstairs by the maid, and then through a closed door and down a passage, which led to the nursery, a room that overlooked the grounds at the back of the house, comfortably furnished with rather a shabby lot of furniture, and much too warm. No wonder, thought Florence; there were no windows open, and there was a quite unnecessary fire in the old-fashioned grate too.

Phoebe was sitting at the table, a painting book and a paintbox before her, and opposite her was an elderly woman with a round, pasty face and beady eyes. She got up as they went in, wished Mr Fitzgibbon a good afternoon and stared at Florence.

He brought his considerable charm to bear upon her, so after a moment she relaxed, nodded a greeting to

Florence and told Phoebe to say 'how do you do?' like a little lady.

'Hello,' said Phoebe, and went back to her painting. She would have been a pretty child but her illness had given her the look of an under-nourished waif, with eyes too big for her face and no colour in her cheeks.

Mr Fitzgibbon wasted no time. 'And how is the tipping and tapping going?'

'Well, sir, we don't bother with it—Phoebe doesn't like it, poor little lamb; she's happy to stay in this nice warm room with her old nanny, aren't you, love?'

Phoebe didn't answer her, but after a moment looked sideways at Florence. 'Who's she?'

'I've come to look at you and Sister Napier is here to help me. Dr Gibbs will be here directly.'

'I shan't,' said Phoebe.

Florence pulled out an armchair and sat down beside her. 'Why not?' she asked cheerfully. 'Do tell.'

'Just because . . .'

'We've come a long way,' said Florence, 'and Mr Fitzgibbon is a very busy man. Still, if you won't there's nothing for us to do but get into the car and drive all the way back to London.' She had picked up a paint-brush and was colouring an elephant bright red.

'Elephants aren't red!' said the child scornfully.

'No. But it's nice to do things wrong sometimes, isn't it? Roses are red . . . do you go into the garden each day and smell them?'

'I'm too ill.'

'That's why Mr Fitzgibbon has come to see you; he'll examine you, and perhaps he'll tell you that you're not so ill any more, and then you can go into the garden.'

Florence finished the elephant and started to paint a zebra with purple stripes.

'I'm very highly strung,' said Phoebe, 'did you know?'

'I've often wondered what that meant—do you suppose you swing from the ceiling?'

Phoebe chuckled. 'I like you. I didn't like the other nurse—I bit her.'

'Ah, but you won't need to bite anyone today because you're getting better.'

Mr Fitzgibbon had been talking to Nanny, but he turned to look at Florence now. He asked, 'Aren't you afraid to get bitten, Florence?'

'Me, sir? Not in the least; in any case, I always bite back.'

He laughed, but Nanny frowned, and it was just as well that the door opened then and Dr Gibbs came in. He was elderly with a nice kind face, and he greeted Mr Fitzgibbon warmly.

'This is Sister Napier, who has replaced Sister Brice, and, since we're all here, shall we have an examination and then discuss the situation later? We are to spend the night. Sister Napier will carry out the tipping and tapping in the morning and let me know what progress has been made. I understand that it has been discontinued.'

'Yes, well, I'll tell you about that.' Dr Gibbs shook Florence's hand. 'If Nanny will allow us we can go into Phoebe's room...'

Phoebe was by no means an easy little patient; the examination took twice as long as it needed to, while Florence used all her patience and ingenuity to keep the child reasonably calm and still. The two men went away presently, leaving her to pacify Phoebe as she dressed her again and then handed her back to a suspicious Nanny.

Florence explained that she would have to rouse Phoebe in the morning and bore meekly the other woman's resentment. 'I'm sorry,' said Florence, 'but Mr Fitzgibbon has told me to do this, and he is in charge of the child. I'm sure you want the best possible treatment for her.'

She bade the still complaining child goodbye for the moment and found her way downstairs. Poor little Phoebe was an ill child and she need not have been—given a longer period in hospital and the proper treatment, she would have had a chance to live longer. Florence thought that once they had gone again Nanny would do exactly what she wanted, and any treatment Mr Fitzgibbon had ordered would be ignored.

She wasn't sure where she should go or what she should do—there was no sign of anyone. The two men would be discussing their findings or having tea with the Villierses, which reminded her that a cup of tea would be welcome. As there was no one in sight, she walked through the hall and out of the front door, and strolled along the carefully tended paths; they looked as though no one ever walked along them . . .

Mr Fitzgibbon, standing at the drawing-room window, listening to Mrs Villiers's peevish voice assuring him that she was far too sensitive to see that the treatment he had ordered was properly carried out and adding a list of her own ailments, allowed his eyes to stray to Florence, strolling along in the afternoon sunshine. Her copper hair glowed under the neat cap, and he thought that even in her severe uniform she looked exactly right in a rose garden.

He heard Mrs Villiers say fretfully, 'Well, I suppose we had better have a cup of tea. Do sit down, Mr Fitzgibbon, and you, Dr Gibbs. I suppose your nurse will want tea?'

'I am sure that Sister Napier would like that. I see that she is walking in the garden.'

'Archie, go and fetch her, will you?'

Conversation over tea was constrained, and Phoebe wasn't mentioned, but when the teacups had been carried away Mr Fitzgibbon observed, at his most bland, 'If I may I shall take Sister Napier into the garden and brief her as to tomorrow morning, and then perhaps we may have a talk about Phoebe.'

They were well away from the house when he asked, 'Well?'

'Well what, sir? If we're talking about Phoebe I think it's a crying shame that her treatment has been so neglected. If it had been carried out properly and she could have gone back into hospital . . . Can't you make them?' she asked fiercely.

'My dear girl, short of living here and sharing Phoebe's nursery, I see no way of altering things. I have suggested that they employ a nurse to care for the child. Mrs Villiers tells me, however, that Nanny wouldn't agree to that and she categorically refuses to discuss it. Dr Gibbs does what he can but, as you know, one cannot insist on treatment against the patient's wishes or, in the case of Phoebe, her parents'.'

'Nanny is angry that I must disturb Phoebe tomorrow morning.'

'I thought she might be. Would you like me to come along too?'

'At six o'clock in the morning?' She turned to look up at him. 'That wouldn't do at all.'

'I want to be away by nine o'clock. Dr Gibbs will be here at half-past eight—you will be ready?'

'Yes, sir.'

'Do you suppose,' asked Mr Fitzgibbon smoothly, 'that when there is no one around you might stop calling me sir with every other breath?'

Florence considered this. 'No, it wouldn't do at all.'

'It makes me feel elderly.'

'Nonsense, you're not in the least elderly. Do you suppose I'm to dine with you this evening, or have something on a tray?'

He stopped to look down at her with an air of cold surprise which quite shook her. 'Do you imagine that I would allow that? I am surprised at you even suggesting such an idea.'

'Well, I dare say you are, but Mrs Villiers wouldn't be...'

'Let us not waste time talking about her.' They turned to walk back towards the house. 'I'm operating tomorrow afternoon at two o'clock. Theatre Sister is on holiday, so I shall want you to scrub.'

'You tell me now!' exclaimed Florence. 'Really, you are—— '

'Yes?' asked Mr Fitzgibbon softly.

'Never mind, sir. What are you going to do?'

'A lobectomy—you can manage that?'

'I shall do my best, sir.' She spoke sweetly, but her blue eyes flashed and the colour came into her cheeks.

'You are quite startlingly beautiful when you're cross,' said Mr Fitzgibbon, and opened the doors into the drawing-room so that she might go ahead of him.

She had been given a room near the nursery. It was pleasant enough, given that it was furnished with the impersonal style of a hotel bedroom. There was a bathroom next door, and she whiled away the hour before dinner lying in a very hot bath, thinking about Mr Fitzgibbon. The thoughts were wispy—odds and ends of conversations, the manner in which he could change from a pleasant companion to a reserved consultant, the expert way in which he handled his car, the way he had tackled what had appeared to be the hopeless task of freeing the man in the truck. 'I shall end up liking him if I go on like this,' said Florence, peering at her lobster-red person in the bathroom mirror.

Later, in bed and half asleep, she went over the evening. Dinner had been very formal, and the sight of Mrs Villiers in black chiffon and sequins had made her very aware of her uniform, even though it was the pristine one she had packed. The conversation had been stilted, with Mrs Villiers talking about her delicate constitution, her husband making very little effort to take part in the conversation, and Mr Fitzgibbon, with his beautiful manners, saying the right things at the right time. As for herself, she had answered when spoken to, listened to Mrs Villiers's grumbles with what she privately called her listening face, and allowed her thoughts to wander. They wandered all over the place and ended up at Mr Fitzgibbon as she fell asleep.

They left at nine o'clock the next morning, and Florence heaved a sigh of relief as Mr Fitzgibbon turned the car on to the road. The morning so far had been horrendous. Phoebe had been a handful, and Nanny had made her worse. Florence had longed to tell her that her cosseting of the child was doing more harm than good, but she guessed that Mr Fitzgibbon had already made that plain. She had eaten a solitary breakfast while he and Dr Gibbs had talked to the Villierses. She stole a look at his stern profile, and decided not to speak until spoken to.

They were more than halfway to the motorway before he said anything.

'We could have done a great deal for that child. Dr Gibbs will continue to urge them to let her go into hospital, but I'm afraid that by the time he does it may be too late to be of much help.'

Florence, despite her kicked shins, agreed with him. 'Poor scrap,' she said.

'You did very well, Florence, and I'm sorry that you weren't treated with better manners.'

'That didn't matter.'

He gave her a quick glance. 'You're a kind girl and you haven't uttered a single grumble. We'll stop at Milton Keynes and have a pot of coffee.'

They joined the M1 presently, travelling for the most part in silence. Florence was quite glad of that: it gave her a chance to check up on her theatre technique.

They stopped at the Post House in Milton Keynes and had their coffee and a plate of buns, not hurrying, and talking in a desultory fashion, and, although they didn't say much for the rest of the journey, Florence found the silence comfortable. Perhaps their relationship was getting on to a more friendly footing. She was surprised to realise that she very much hoped so.

CHAPTER FIVE

MR FITZGIBBON left his consulting-rooms within minutes of arriving, staying only long enough to check Mrs Keane's carefully written messages and go through his post, leaving Florence with the advice that she should be at Colbert's not later than a quarter-past one. 'I have my own instruments there,' he went on, 'but it would be as well for you to check everything before we start.'

Well, of course it would, she agreed silently, and what about her lunch? He had gone without another word.

She said rather worriedly to Mrs Keane, 'Do you suppose I dare pop over to Mrs Twist's and ask her for a sandwich? She doesn't like me going there during the day...'

'I thought of that, dear.' Mrs Keane's cosy voice sounded pleased with itself. 'I bought some sausage rolls for you as I came in this morning. I remembered how poor Sister Brice would come back from somewhere or other, quite famished. I've got the kettle on; we'll have a cup of tea, and I'll eat my sandwiches at the same time and you can tell me all about it.'

Before she went to catch the bus to Colbert's Florence took a look at the appointments book. There were two patients for later that afternoon. She reckoned that Mr Fitzgibbon would have finished before four o'clock, but there were still his instruments to check before they went down to be sterilised and repacked. The first patient was booked for five o'clock; with luck she would be back at the consulting-rooms by then. She joined the queue for the bus and wondered just how quickly she would be able to change back into uniform.

Although she had worked as Staff Nurse in Theatre for some months, she felt uncertain about her reception, but she need not have worried. The staff nurse on duty was newly qualified and nervous.

'I'm glad it's you,' she confided as Florence got into her theatre kit, 'he scares me stiff, and he looks at you...'

'Well, yes,' agreed Florence, and thought that his eyes were rather nice; they could, of course, look like grey steel, but on the other hand they could look warm and amused. 'Now I'd better lay up my trolley.'

The anaesthetist remembered her as she walked in with the trolley, and he nodded to her in a friendly fashion. 'Hello, Florence, how nice to see you back. No chance of you staying with us?'

He checked his patient and settled down on his stool, and when she shook her head observed, 'Working for Fitzgibbon, aren't you? He's a lucky chap!'

Florence's lovely eyes crinkled in a smile behind her mask; a pity Mr Fitzgibbon wasn't there to hear that. He came a moment later, towering over everyone in his green gown. He wished everyone an affable good afternoon, and got down to work. He had his registrar with him and a houseman, rather timidly assisting, very much in awe of his chief. He had no need to be; Mr Fitzgibbon shed the light of his good humour over everyone there, so that the houseman became quite efficient and the little staff nurse, who was good at her job, forgot to be nervous of him. He worked unhurriedly and with the ease of long practice, and Florence, all the well-remembered routine taking over, handed instruments seconds before he held out a hand for them. All the while he carried on a casual conversation with the other men, so that the atmosphere, which had been rather fraught when he had first come in, became decidedly relaxed. In all, reflected Florence, getting out of the gown, a pleasant afternoon. She was carefully checking his instruments, which one of the nurses was washing before sending them to be sterilised, and she was still in her green theatre smock, when he came back into Theatre.

'How long will you be?' he asked.

'Me? Oh, fifteen minutes, sir. I'll be back in time for the first patient.'

'Make sure it is fifteen minutes—I'll be outside in the forecourt.'

'There's no...' She caught his eye, grey steel. 'Very well, sir,' she said, outwardly meek.

'He's never going to take you back with him?' said the little staff nurse.

'Well, I have to be at his consulting-rooms for the first patient, and I might get held up catching a bus,' said Florence practically.

She finished what she was doing calmly, got back into her dress and went down to the forecourt.

He was there, leaning on the car's bonnet, reading the first edition of the evening paper. He folded it away tidily and opened her door. Sitting beside her before starting the engine, he observed, 'You did very well, Florence.'

Her, 'Thank you, sir,' was uttered with just the right amount of meekness.

There was still a little time before the patient would arrive; she was pleased to see that Mrs Keane had the tea-tray ready and surprised when that lady said blithely, 'Tea is made, Mr Fitzgibbon, and I popped out for some of those biscuits you like. How handy the telephone is, to be sure, otherwise I wouldn't have known when you were coming back. I'll bring you a cup...'

'Thank you, Mrs Keane. The second patient has an appointment for half-past five, hasn't he? When you've shown him in, go home. Florence can do whatever else is necessary.'

'Well, if she doesn't mind...'

'Of course I don't mind; there'll be little enough to do anyway.' She eyed the biscuits hungrily. 'I'll get changed before I have my tea...'

Mr Fitzgibbon paused at the door. 'Did you have lunch?' he wanted to know.

'Mrs Keane was kind enough to get some sausage rolls for me this morning.'

'Sausage rolls?' He eyed her shapely person thoughtfully. 'An insufficient diet for one of your build, Florence.'

If he heard her indignant gasp as he turned away he gave no sign.

She had time for three cups of tea and almost all of the biscuits before the patient arrived, a youngish woman with her husband. She was a little frightened, and it was fearfully difficult to get clear answers to Mr Fitzgibbon's gently put questions. Florence, in attendance, reflected that he must be a kind man under his reserved manner. She mulled over the surprising information Mrs Keane had given her over their tea; he didn't only have a large out-patients clinic at Colbert's and operate there twice a week, but he also had another clinic in Bethnal Green, which dealt with the sad regiments of the homeless, sent to him from various charities. So many of them refused to go to a hospital, but the clinic was a different matter. He had willing helpers too—retired nurses, local doctors, social workers. 'Don't you ever mention it,' warned Mrs

Keane. 'He never talks about it to anyone. He has to tell me, of course, because I keep his notes and do the bills and the rent and so forth for him. He's helped a good many there, I can tell you; gives them money, finds them jobs, and sometimes helps get them somewhere to live. I don't know how he finds the time, and him with a busy social life too.'

Florence showed the patient and her husband out, saw Mrs Keane on her way and, observant of Mr Fitzgibbon's bell, showed in the last patient.

An elderly, rather shabby man, but very neat; his manners were nice too. He wished her a polite good afternoon, volunteered his name—Mr Clarke—and sat down with the air of one expecting to wait.

'There's Mr Clarke, sir,' said Florence, sliding into the consulting-room.

'Ah, yes. Show him in, Florence, will you? I shan't be needing you for the moment. You could start tidying up.'

She gave him a cross look. Tidying up was none of his business—she was well aware of what had to be done and when. He was writing something, and without looking up he murmured, 'You wished to say something?'

'Yes, but I won't,' said Florence, and swept back into the waiting-room to usher Mr Clarke in.

As she closed the door she heard Mr Fitzgibbon's voice, friendly and calm. 'Mr Clarke, I'm so glad that you could come...'

She went and looked out of the window for a few moments, and then began her clearing up. There wasn't much to do. She put things ready for the morning and went to look at the appointments book. There was a slip of paper tucked into it and she looked at it idly. It was a note in Mr Fitzgibbon's scrawling handwriting, addressed to Mrs Keane, telling her to make an appointment for Mr Clarke, who should by rights have attended his out-patients clinic at Colbert's, but, owing to family circumstances, was unable to do so. 'No fees,' it ended.

Florence put it back where she had found it. It was getting very hard to dislike Mr Fitzgibbon.

She was roused from her thoughts by his voice on Mrs Keane's intercom, bidding her return. Mr Clarke had to be weighed, his blood-pressure taken, his pulse recorded and his respirations noted, and while she did these things she could see that the nice little man was upset and quite determined not to show it. Her small chores done, she went away again and presently showed him out before going into the examination-room to replace towels and the couch cover, clean up generally and stow everything that had been used in the laundry bag. She didn't hurry over this; the evening stretched before her and, although it was a lovely summer one, she was tired, mentally as well as physically. She would eat whatever supper Mrs Twist put before her and go to bed with a book. The appointment book was crammed for the next day and she felt reasonably sure that she wouldn't be able to get the evening train home. That couldn't be helped; she would go on Saturday morning, and in the afternoon she would take her mother into Sherborne and they would buy the washing-machine. Florence fingered the pay envelope in the pocket of her uniform and decided that, uncertain hours or not, it was worth it.

There was no sign of Mr Fitzgibbon and, since she was quite finished, she tapped on his door and went in. 'Is there anything more you would like done, sir?' she asked.

He closed the folder in which he had been writing. 'Nothing—I think we've crammed as much into today as we can, don't you? We've earned ourselves a meal. I've some work to finish here and I must go home. I'll call for you at Mrs Twist's house in an hour's time.'

'Are you inviting me out to dinner, Mr Fitzgibbon?' Her voice was tart.

He looked up briefly. 'Well, of course I am; had I not made myself plain?'

She hesitated: the invitation had sounded more like an order; on the other hand, the dinner he was offering would surely be more appetising than Mrs Twist's reliable but uninspired cooking. 'Thank you, sir, I should like to come.'

'Good, and for God's sake stop calling me sir.'

'Very well, Mr Fitzgibbon,' and then a little shyly, 'Do I need to dress up?'

His fine mouth twitched. 'No, no, there's a nice little place just off Wigmore Street, five minutes' walk from here.' He looked up and smiled at her, a slow, comforting smile. 'You must be tired.'

'I'll be ready in an hour, Mr Fitzgibbon.' She whisked away, very quickly got out of uniform and sped back to Mrs Twist, ready with apologies for not eating the supper which that good lady would have prepared for her, but she had no need of them: Mr Fitzgibbon had telephoned, and her landlady met her with a simpering smile and the opinion that Mr Fitzgibbon was a gentleman right enough, and was Florence likely to be late back?

'Most unlikely,' said Florence in a matter-of-fact manner. 'We're both tired and tomorrow is booked solid. I may have to stay Friday night and catch an early train home on Saturday morning.'

'Perhaps he'll drive you home again?' suggested Mrs Twist, a woman with a romantic turn of mind.

'Most unlikely, Mrs Twist. Would you mind if I had my bath now instead of this evening?'

'You go ahead, and make the best of yourself,' advised Mrs Twist.

Advice which Florence intended to take. Nicely refreshed from her bath, she examined her wardrobe, searching for something suitable to wear to a nice little place within five minutes' walk. It was a pity, she reflected, that she had no idea what a nice little place consisted of in Mr Fitzgibbon's mind. She decided on a leaf-green crêpe dress with a square neckline and a little matching jacket, piled her copper hair into a chignon, thrust her feet into white sandals, found the little white handbag and put all that she might need into it, and took a last look at herself in the old-fashioned wardrobe mirror. Not being a conceited girl, she decided that she looked all right, thanking heaven that it was a fine evening and that she wouldn't need to take a coat. She hadn't got a suitable one anyway. She would get one on Saturday, she promised herself, and went downstairs, a few minutes early.

Mr Fitzgibbon was in Mrs Twist's front parlour, making himself agreeable to that lady. He had changed into a lighter suit and his tie was slightly less sombre than usual, and gold cuff-links gleamed discreetly from snow-white cuffs. He looked, thought Florence, extremely handsome; no wonder that Eleanor woman was after him. He stood up as she went in.

'Ah, Florence, punctual as always.' He studied her person without appearing to do so, bade Mrs Twist farewell and ushered her outside. 'You don't mind a very short walk? The car is outside the consulting-rooms if you would prefer to drive?'

'I'd like a walk. We don't have much time to take walks, do we?'

'Very little. Do you walk a lot at home?'

'Oh, yes. Miles—I sometimes cycle, though. Father has two villages in the parish as well as Gussage Tollard; when I'm at home I often have to help out with the Mothers' Union and choir practice, and then the bike comes in handy.'

'Do you like country life?'

'I was born and brought up in the vicarage—I went away to boarding-school, but only to Sherborne. I hated London when I came to Colbert's to train.'

'It is hardly a good part in which to live.'

They were walking through the quiet, dignified streets, and she looked round her. 'Well, no, but this is quite different; one could live in any of these streets and be quite content. Though I'd miss the country...'

'A weekend cottage in the country would settle that question, wouldn't it?'

Florence laughed. 'Very nicely. I must look round for a wealthy man with a house round about here and another one in some pretty village.'

He said dreamily, 'There are plenty of wealthy men living in and around this area...'

'I'm sure that there are, only I don't have the chance to meet any of them.'

She looked up at him and laughed. 'Isn't it nice to talk nonsense sometimes?' They were in a narrow side-street, and a moment later he ushered her down some steps into a quite small restaurant, its tables covered in snowy linen and set with gleaming cutlery and lighted by candles. It was fairly full, and Florence was relieved to see that her dress would pass muster. She sat down and glanced around her unselfconsciously with frank pleasure. It was an attractive place with white walls, upon which hung some rather nice flower paintings, and the seats were comfortable, the tables not too close together and the waiter, when he came, most attentive.

The menu was impressive and there were no prices upon it, a fact which left her in some doubt as to what to order. Small it might be, but she had a suspicion that it was expensive.

Mr Fitzgibbon, watching her from under drooping lids, smiled to himself.

'I don't know about you,' he observed, 'but I'm hungry. How about crab mousse to start with, noisettes of lamb—they do a splendid sauce with them—and we can choose a sweet later?'

Much relieved, she agreed at once, and agreed again when he suggested a dry sherry while they waited. 'This is a delightful place—why, you wouldn't even know it was here, would you?'

He understood her. 'Nicely hidden away and quiet.'

For something to say she asked, 'I expect you've been here before?'

'Several times.' He smiled at her across the table; she really looked charming sitting there opposite him, the candlelight turning her hair to burnished gold. The dress, he decided, was by no means new or in the forefront of fashion, and she had no jewellery, only a plain gold chain and her watch. He found himself comparing her with Eleanor, who had phoned that evening and demanded that he should take her to some party or other. He had drifted into a casual friendship with her over the years, and although he wasn't in love with her he had found himself wondering if he might marry her. He wanted a wife, a home life and children, but not with Eleanor; the certainty of that had been in his mind for several weeks, although he had ignored it. Now, watching Florence, he acknowledged it.

He began a trivial conversation, touching on a variety of subjects. Over the lamb he asked casually, 'You like reading?'

She popped some delicious garden peas into her mouth. 'Oh, yes. Anything I can lay hands on...'

'Poetry?'

'Well, yes, I like John Donne and the Brownings— oh, and Herrick; I'd rather read a book, though.'

'*Jane Eyre*?' he asked with a twinkle. '*Pride and Prejudice, Wuthering Heights*, anything by—what is her name?—M M Kaye?'

Florence speared a baby carrot. 'However did you know? Yes, I read all those. I like gentle books, if you see what I mean.'

'Yes, I see. You're a gentle girl, Florence. Because you're a parson's daughter?'

She took the remark seriously. 'Yes, probably, but I do have a very nasty temper.'

'So do I, Florence, although I flatter myself that I can control it unless I'm severely provoked.'

'Well, I don't suppose that happens very often,' said Florence comfortably. 'People always seem to do what you want straight away, but, of course, you're important, aren't you?'

She looked up, smiling, and met a steely grey stare. 'Are you buttering me up, Florence?'

She refused to be intimidated. 'Good heavens, no. Why should I do that? Anyway, it's true, and I'm sorry if you're mad at me. Father is always telling me to think before I speak.'

'It is I who should apologise, Florence. Feel free to say what you want without thinking first.'

'Excepting when I'm at work, of course.'

'Having settled the matter, let us turn our attention to a sweet. Biscuit glacé, perhaps, with strawberries? Or a crème brûlée?'

'I'd like the biscuit glacé, please; I can make a crème brûlée at home...'

He ordered, and asked for the cheese board for himself. 'You can cook?'

'Well, of course I can, and I had plenty of opportunity to try out recipes while I was looking after Mother. I suppose all women can cook; it comes naturally, like making beds and ironing shirts.' She was matter-of-fact.

He reflected that he had never had the opportunity of knowing if Eleanor could do any of those things, but it seemed unlikely. He must remember to ask her next time they met. The thought that he was enjoying himself engendered a wish to repeat the occasion.

They had their coffee and walked back presently, and at Mrs Twist's door he took the key from her. 'Do we have to look out for Buster?'

'No, he'll be with Mrs Twist upstairs.' She took back the key. 'Thank you for my dinner, Mr Fitzgibbon; it was a lovely evening.'

'It was a pleasure, Florence.'

He opened the door and she went inside. 'Goodnight, and thank you again.'

His 'Goodnight, Florence,' was quietly said as she closed the door.

She wasn't quite sure what she expected when she got to work the next morning, but it certainly wasn't Mr Fitzgibbon's cold stare and equally cold 'Good morning.' He was seated at his desk, looking so unlike the pleasant companion of the previous evening that the smile faded from her pretty face, and at the first opportunity she sought out Mrs Keane to ask her if she had done or not done something.

'Don't worry, dear,' soothed Mrs Keane, 'I know he's very pleased with your work. Something's on his mind— or someone; that Eleanor, I suppose...'

'Are they engaged or—or anything?'

'No, nor likely to be: he's no more in love with her than I am. He's thirty-six now, and if you ask me he's never been in love—not enough to want to marry. For one thing he's too busy, and for another she'd have to be a girl who could get past that austere manner.'

'He's not always austere,' said Florence, remembering the previous evening.

Mrs Keane gave her a quick look. 'No, dear, but only a few people know that.' She put on the kettle. 'There's time for a cup of tea now if we're quick, before the first patient comes; we can have coffee later. I'll see to the percolator and have the coffee ready, and you can take him a cup then.'

The first patient arrived and Florence turned into an impersonal automaton, doing what was required of her and then melting into the background until she was needed again, carefully not looking higher than Mr Fitzgibbon's firm chin, and when the patient had gone she fetched his coffee and set the cup and saucer down on his desk gently, suppressing a sudden and surprising wish to throw the lot at him. She wasn't at all sure why, but it might have relieved her feelings.

The last patient for the morning had gone when he was called away to the hospital, and half an hour later he rang to say that the afternoon patients would have to be notified that he would be delayed. 'Postpone the first appointment for half an hour,' he told Mrs Keane, 'and the rest for the same time.'

'There goes my chance to get the evening train,' said Florence crossly. 'That's two weekends running. Do you mind if I use the phone to let Mother know?'

'Perhaps that nice Mr Fitzgibbon will drive you down again, love,' said her mother in a pleased voice.

Florence snorted. 'It's the last thing he'll do,' she said snappily, 'and he's not all that nice.'

She was instantly sorry. 'I didn't mean that, Mother. I'm to stay, and I've got my pay packet—we'll go into Sherborne tomorrow afternoon and buy a washing-machine.'

'Oh, darling, how lovely, but I think you should spend your money on some new clothes.'

'Next month, Mother. I must go—see you tomorrow. Let Father know, won't you?'

There were four appointments in the afternoon, and Mr Fitzgibbon took his time over each one of them. Since one patient telephoned to say that she would be unable to come until later in the afternoon, there was a half-hour's wait. Mrs Keane made tea and Florence got as far as she could with the clearing up, but since there were still two patients to come it seemed a waste of time. She took him a cup of tea, outwardly serene and inwardly seething with impatience.

'You will be unable to go home this evening,' remarked Mr Fitzgibbon. 'A pity, but it cannot be helped. Our friend from the truck had a secondary haemorrhage, and it was necessary to take him back to Theatre.'

'Oh, how awful. Will he be all right? Was it his stump?'

'No, the chest wound. I've had another look and found the trouble. He should do now.' He bent his head over the papers on his desk and she went away, feeling that she would have liked to tell him how mean she felt, moaning because she had had to miss her train while all the while he had been dealing with an emergency. She told Mrs Keane while they drank their tea and was comforted by her sensible observation that, since she hadn't known about it, she had no need to feel guilty.

The delayed patient had come for a check-up and took up a mere twenty minutes of Mr Fitzgibbon's time, but the last patient, a middle-aged and timid lady, accompanied by her husband, took up twice that time, partly because before any examination could be done she needed to be soothed and encouraged. Afterwards, when Florence was helping her to dress again, she felt faint, which delayed her departure for even longer. Florence tucked her up on the examination couch and put a comforting arm around her shoulders while she had a little weep. 'Why does it have to be me?' she demanded tearfully. 'I don't even smoke cigarettes. Do you suppose that Mr Fitzgibbon can really cure me?'

'Certainly he can if he said so,' said Florence stoutly, 'and you don't have to worry about the operation; you really won't know anything about it, and you'll be well again within weeks—you heard him say so. Now I'm going to tell him that you're ready, and you'll go back into the consulting-room and he'll explain everything to you. You can ask him any questions that you want to; he's a kind man and very clever.'

'You are a dear, sweet girl, putting up with an old woman's nonsense.' She patted Florence's arm. 'Shall I see you again?'

'Oh, yes, in a few weeks' time when you come for a check-up after surgery. I shall look forward to seeing you then.'

There was quite a lot to do once the elderly pair had left. Florence took herself off to the examination-room and began to set it to rights, and then put her head round the door to ask if Mr Fitzgibbon would like a cup of coffee.

He refused, still working at his desk, and as she withdrew her head the phone rang. 'Answer that, will you,' he asked her, 'and see who it is?'

Eleanor, thought Florence, and she was right. The piercing voice sounded petulant and demanding, and asked to speak to Mr Fitzgibbon.

'Miss Paton wishes to speak to you, sir.'

He growled something softly and took the phone from her. As Florence went out of the room, closing the door very, very slowly, she heard him say, 'Eleanor, I am extremely busy...' She held the door-handle so that there was still a crack before she closed it, and nodded her head with satisfaction at his, 'No, quite impossible, I shall be working...!'

Mr Fitzgibbon, watching the door-handle soundlessly turning, smiled, paying not the slightest attention to Eleanor's petulant voice.

When Florence went back presently to say that everything was attended to and did he wish her to remain any longer? he lifted his head from his writing to tell her baldly that he needed nothing more and she had no need to stay. He wished her a good night in a voice which suggested that he had no wish to enter into conversation of any kind, and picked up his pen again.

Florence's 'Goodnight,' was crisp. He might at least have expressed regret at her having to miss her evening train. I hope she pesters him to take her out and makes him spend a lot of money at some glitzy restaurant, thought Florence, going back to one of Mrs Twist's wholesome suppers.

Mr Fitzgibbon went home to the charming little Georgian house not ten minutes' drive from his rooms, changed into elderly, beautifully tailored tweeds, told Crib, the elderly man who ran his home with the help of his wife, that he would be back on Sunday night, whistled to Monty, that dog of no known breed, and got back into his car.

Once out of London, he took the A30 and just over two hours later slowed the car as he reached the first grey stone thatched cottages of Mells. It was a small village with a lovely church, a manor-house and a cluster of these same cottages in a charming group dominated by the church and the village inn. Mr Fitzgibbon drove through the centre of the village, and half a mile along a narrow lane turned the car through an open gate and stopped before a low, rambling house built of the same grey and yellow stone as the cottages, but with a red-tiled roof. The front door stood open and he was met on the doorstep by a short, stout woman with a round rosy face and grey hair screwed up into a fierce bun.

'There you are, Mr Alexander, right on time, too. Good thing you phoned when you did—I had time to get Mr Letts to come up with the nicest piece of steak for your supper.' She paused and he bent to hug her.

'Just what I need, Nanny, and how nice to see you.' He let Monty out of the car and they all went indoors, through the stone-flagged hall to a low-ceilinged room with a great inglenook and lattice windows. Doors opened on to the garden behind the house, a lovely place, a riot of roses and summer flowers, with a wide lawn leading down to a narrow stream.

'You're on your own?' asked Nanny unnecessarily.

'Yes, Nanny...'

'Doesn't like the country, does she, that Miss Paton?'

He said evenly, 'No, I'm afraid it isn't quite the life for her.' He had sat down in a great chair and Monty had flopped at his feet. Presently he went on, 'You were quite right, Nanny...'

'Of course I was, Mr Alexander. You just wait until the right girl comes along.'

'She has, but she doesn't know it yet.'

Nanny sat down on a small chair opposite him. She didn't say a word, only waited.

'She's a parson's daughter, a nurse, and she works for me.'

'She likes you?'

'I think so, but not at first, and even now I catch her looking at me as though she wasn't sure of that. On the other hand...'

'Give her time, Mr Alexander.' Nanny got up. 'I'll get your supper; you must be famished, and that nice dog of yours.'

He was up early the next morning and, with Monty beside him, inspected the garden before breakfast. The thought that he was barely an hour's drive away from Florence's home was persistent in his mind but he refused to listen to it. After breakfast he went into the village, where he met the rector and returned with him to have coffee at the rectory. The rector was a keen gardener and the hours passed pleasantly. After lunch he stretched out on the lawn and slept until Nanny called him in to tea. Then he and Monty took themselves off for a long walk before spending a convivial hour in the Talbot Arms. In the evening, after the splendid dinner Nanny put before him, he sat in the lovely drawing-room, thinking about Florence. At length he got up to go to bed, saw Monty into his basket in the kitchen, locked up and turned off the lights before going up the oak staircase to his room. The night was clear and there was a waning moon. He stood by the open window, wondering if Florence was looking at the same moon, and then laughed wryly. 'I'm behaving like a lovesick boy,' he muttered, 'and more than likely she doesn't give a second thought to me...'

Florence wasn't looking at the moon, she was in bed and asleep, but she had from time to time during the day thought about him. She had taken herself to task over this. 'We haven't anything in common except our work,' she told Charlie Brown, snoozing on her bed. 'He lives in London, though I don't know where—in some hideously expensive modern flat, I suppose—and he likes expensive restaurants and big cars, and he hardly ever laughs. And he never looks at me...'

She was wrong, of course, about that.

It was at Sunday lunch that her mother asked, 'I suppose that nice Mr Fitzgibbon has to work at the weekend?'

'I've no idea,' said Florence, 'but I shouldn't think so—he must have a private life.'

'A great many firm friends if he's not married, I expect,' suggested Mrs Napier. 'Handsome single men are always in great demand.'

Florence was filled with a sudden fierce dislike of that. She said, 'I dare say; I really don't know anything about him, Mother.' As she spoke she wished that she did. Where did he go when he left the consulting-rooms, for instance? Did he have parents and live with them, or brothers and sisters? And his friends—surely there must

be others than the horrid Eleanor? She could think of
no way of finding out, and suddenly she wanted to know
quite badly. She reminded herself once again that she
was getting too interested in him, and spent the rest of
the day gardening with unnecessary energy, and,
although she hated leaving home that evening, there was
a spark of excitement deep down inside her at the idea
of seeing him again.

She went to work a little earlier than usual, a habit
she had formed on a Monday morning, to make sure
that everything was just so. She was rearranging flowers
in a bowl kept filled throughout the year in the waiting-
room when Mr Fitzgibbon came in.

A small wave of pleasure at the sight of him left her
feeling surprised; there was no particular reason why she
should be glad to see him—he hadn't been over-friendly
on Friday evening. She bade him good morning and was
relieved when he answered her with brisk cheerfulness
and a quick smile. He didn't stop to talk; he went straight
to his consulting-room and began on his post, so that
when Mrs Keane arrived he called her in at once to take
his letters. He saw two patients and then took himself
off to Colbert's, leaving Florence and Mrs Keane to get
ready for the busy afternoon ahead of them.

Mrs Keane, her hands poised over her typewriter,
waited until his footsteps had ceased in the house before
observing, 'I wonder what is making him so thoughtful?
And absent-minded—he usually rattles off his letters,
but this morning he kept going off into a world of his
own. There's something on his mind...'

'That Eleanor—she phoned on Friday evening,' said
Florence, tucking a clean sheet on the couch and raising
her voice through the open door. 'But he said he couldn't

take her out. Do you suppose he's met someone he likes better?'

Mrs Keane bent over her notebook. 'I've no doubt of it,' she said with quiet satisfaction.

CHAPTER SIX

THE day's work went smoothly; Mr Fitzgibbon returned directly after lunch and the whole afternoon was taken up with his patients. Usually Mrs Keane booked appointments so that there was a brief lull halfway through the afternoon, enabling them to have a cup of tea, but today there was no let-up, and by five o'clock Florence was tired and a little cross beneath her seemingly composed appearance, and the prospect of the evening spent alone in her room was uninviting. Mrs Twist would be out, spending the evening with friends, and there would only be Buster for company. Showing the last patient out with smiling friendliness, she decided to go out for the evening herself. She had money—not a great deal, but quite enough to take her to some quiet little restaurant where she could get a modest meal. She would have to get a bus to Oxford Street, where there was bound to be somewhere to suit her taste. She bustled around, drank her tea thankfully, took a cup to an unsmiling Mr Fitzgibbon, and, everything being in apple-pie order, asked if there was anything else he wished her to do.

He looked up briefly. 'No, thank you, Florence; enjoy your evening. Are you going out?'

She beamed at him. 'Yes—for a meal. Goodnight, sir.'

He bade her goodnight in a cool voice and sat looking at the closed door after she had gone. It was, he argued to himself, most irritating that the girl treated him in such a manner; he had no idea what she really thought of him. At times he thought that she liked him, and then she withdrew, becoming a cross between tolerant youth making allowances for middle age and a waspish young woman ready to answer back. He sighed, admitting at last to himself that he wanted Florence for his wife but that persuading her to be of like mind would probably be a delicate undertaking. Mr Fitzgibbon sat back and considered how best to set about the matter, unaware that kindly providence was about to lend him a hand.

Florence let herself into Mrs Twist's house, fed Buster, inspected the corned-beef salad in the fridge for her supper, put it back and went to her room to change. It was well past six o'clock but she took the opportunity to have a bath, since Mrs Twist was prone to remind her that hot water cost money so that she felt compelled to have a shower when that lady was home. Now she luxuriated at some length in an extravagant amount of hot water, dressed unhurriedly, coiled her hair in a smooth chignon, made sure that she had her key and enough money, and left the house. Outside on the pavement, she remembered that Mr Fitzgibbon had still been in his rooms when she had left and, for all she knew, he might still be there. She had no wish to encounter him and, remembering Mrs Twist telling her that there was a short cut which would bring her out almost by Cavendish Square, well past the consulting-rooms, she decided to take it.

It was a narrow street with small, neat houses on either side; there were cars parked on one side of it, but otherwise it was empty. It was later than she had intended, for she had dawdled over her dressing and spent ten minutes sitting on the stairs with Buster, who had been feeling lonely, but the June evening was still light and would be for some time to come. She walked on, hardly noticing that the houses were becoming shabby, for she was allowing her imagination full rein; Mr Fitzgibbon would be spending his evening with Eleanor, no doubt; she didn't think that he was very in love with her, though, but Florence guessed that she was too clever to give him a chance to know that. Men, she thought, might be very clever and all that, but they could be singularly blind at times. She looked around her then and saw how the street had changed from neatness to a neglected, rubbish-strewn thoroughfare with paint peeling off the front doors and grubby curtains at the windows. She must have mistaken Mrs Twist's directions, and she was relieved to see a main street ahead of her, busy with cars. She stepped out more briskly and at the same time became aware that she was being followed.

She didn't turn round, nor did she increase her pace, although it was the one thing she would have liked to do. Common sense told her that she was near enough to the end of the street to scream for help if she needed to, and to show unease might spur on whoever it was behind her... Getting closer, too...

She hadn't realised how close: a large, heavy hand caught her by the shoulder and forced her to stop.

Mr Fitzgibbon, on the way home and the last in the queue at the traffic-lights, looked round him idly, marvelling for the hundredth time how it was possible for such neglected, down-at-heel streets to be cheek by jowl with the elegance around them. It was then that providence, metaphorically speaking, tapped him on one massive shoulder so that his glance strayed into the street alongside the car. He saw that copper head of hair immediately; he also saw that its owner was in difficulties. He was out of the car and into the street, oblivious of anything other than the need to get to Florence as fast as possible. For a man of his size, he was a quick mover. He was very nearly there when he saw her kick hard backwards with sufficiently good result to make the man yelp. He was on him then, removing him with a great arm, shaking him like a terrier shook a rat.

'I advise you not to do that again, my man,' said Mr Fitzgibbon without heat, 'or it will be the worse for you.' He let him go and watched him run back down the street before he turned to Florence.

'And what the hell were you doing, strolling down this back street, asking for trouble—a great girl like you...?'

Florence gulped. Being called a great girl in that coldly furious voice was upsetting; worse, it sparked off the temper her parents had been at pains to teach her to control from an early age. She was a bit shaken and a trifle pale, and her voice wobbled just a little, but more with temper than fright. She said with great dignity, 'I am not a great girl...'

'We'll argue about that in the car—I'll be had up for obstruction...'

He took her by the arm and marched her along willy-nilly. 'I don't wish——' she began, but he stowed her into the car without a word, got in himself and drove on.

'A miracle that there is no traffic or police around,' he observed grimly. It wasn't a miracle but providence, of course.

He took the car round Cavendish Square and into Regent Street, turning off into side-streets before he reached Piccadilly and coming out at the lower end of Park Lane and so into Knightsbridge.

Florence, who had sat silently fuming, said, 'This is Knightsbridge; why are you bringing me here?'

He didn't answer but turned into a quiet side-street lined with rather grand houses, and presently turned again under an archway into a narrow tree-lined street. The houses were smaller here but very elegant, painted white, their front doors gleaming with black paint. He stopped before the end house, got out, opened her door and invited her to get out.

'No,' said Florence, and then, catching the look in his eye, she got out, but once on the pavement she didn't budge. 'Why have you brought me here? And where is it anyway? I'm obliged to you for your—your help just now, but...' she paused, pink in the face, her blue eyes flashing '...a great girl like me can look after herself.' She frowned because she suspected that she had got the grammar wrong somewhere.

Mr Fitzgibbon smiled, not very nicely, took her by the arm in a gentle but firm grasp, and marched her to his front door. Crib opened it, and if he was surprised he showed no sign of it, but bade his master a good evening and added a respectful good evening to Florence.

'Ah, Crib, this is Miss Napier, my practice nurse; she has had an unfortunate encounter in the street. Will you ask Mrs Crib to show her where she can tidy herself?' And, when Crib bustled off down the narrow hall and through a baize door at its end, Mr Fitzgibbon observed in an aloof way, 'You will be better when you have had a drink and a meal.'

'I feel perfectly all right,' snapped Florence, but she couldn't go on because a tall thin woman in a severe grey dress had come through the door and was advancing towards them.

'Good evening, sir,' she smiled at Florence, 'and good evening to you too, miss. If you will come with me?'

She led Florence, speechless and cross, up the graceful little staircase to one side of the hall. 'I hear you've had some kind of accident, miss,' she remarked as they reached the landing. 'There is a cloakroom in the hall, but I dare say you might like a few minutes' peace and quiet if you have been upset.'

She opened a door and ushered Florence into a charming bedroom; its windows overlooked the back of the house and gave a view of a small pretty garden. It was furnished in maple-wood, carpeted in white and curtained in apricot silk. The bedspread on the small bed was of the same material and so were the lamp-shades, and the walls were a pale tint of the same colour. 'Oh, what a darling room,' said Florence, quite forgetting that she was annoyed.

'One of the guest rooms, miss. The bathroom is through the door there, and if you fancy a nice lie down the *chaise-longue* is very comfortable.'

The housekeeper gave her a kindly smile and went away, and, left to herself, Florence inspected her surroundings more thoroughly. The room was indeed delightful and so was the bathroom, stocked with towels, soap and everything a guest could wish for. Perhaps it had been left ready for a visitor; it seemed a shame to use the soap and one of the fluffy towels so enticingly laid out on one of the glass shelves. However, she had to wash; the man's hand had been dirty, and she could still feel its grimy, sweaty fingers as she had instinctively tried to drag it from her shoulder. She took a look at herself in the wide mirror. There was a dirty mark on her dress and her hair was a mess...!

She went downstairs again some ten minutes later, once more nicely made-up, her fiery head of hair brushed smooth. Her dress had been creased but she couldn't do anything about that, although she had got rid of most of the dirty mark.

There was no one in the hall and she stood, irresolute, at the bottom of the staircase, but only for a moment. Mr Fitzgibbon flung open a door opposite her. 'Come in, come in.' He sounded impatient. 'That's a comfortable chair by the window. What would you like to drink?'

She stood by the door. 'Nothing, thank you, sir. You've been very kind, but I won't trespass upon your time any more.' When he didn't speak she added, 'I'm most grateful . . .'

He crossed the room, took her by the arm and sat her down in the chair he had indicated. 'A glass of sherry,' he observed, and handed it to her. 'There's nothing like it for restoring ill-humour.'

'I am not ill-humoured,' began Florence, determined to make it clear, which, seeing that she was boiling with rage, hardly made sense.

'You are as cross as two sticks,' said Mr Fitzgibbon genially. 'You are also foolish and most regrettably untruthful.'

Florence had taken a sip of sherry and choked on it, but before she could summon breath to utter he had sat down opposite her, a glass in his hand, the picture of good-natured ease. 'When you have your breath back,' he suggested, 'I should like to know why you were in that disreputable street and why, having told me that you were going out for a meal, you had done no such thing. Did he stand you up?'

'Stand me up? Who?'

'You were intending to dine out alone?'

'Well, what's so funny about that? And I wasn't going to dine. How can you be so silly? On my salary? I was going to Oxford Street to McDonald's or somewhere like that.' She added to make things clearer, 'Mrs Twist's out this evening and it was corned beef and tomatoes.'

Mr Fitzgibbon hid a smile. 'Did you need to fib about it? I am afraid I can't quite see...' He watched the lovely pink creep into her face and saw. 'You were afraid that I might think you were fishing for another meal...'

'What a simply horrid thing to say,' she burst out.

'It's the truth,' he pointed out blandly.

'Well, even if it is, you don't have to say it—I mean, you can think it if you want to but you don't have to put it into words.'

She tossed off the sherry in a defiant way, and he got up and refilled her glass. 'Now I want to know why you were wandering around, asking to be mugged. If you intend to go to Oxford Street you could have kept to Wimpole Street until you came to the bus-stop.'

She managed not to blush this time, but she looked so guilty that Mr Fitzgibbon, watching her from beneath his lids, knew that she was about to tell him some more fibs.

'Well,' began Florence, 'Mrs Twist told me about this short-cut, and it was such a nice evening and the street really looked quite respectable when I started. I thought it would make a nice change.'

It sounded a bit thin, and she could see that Mr Fitzgibbon thought it was too, for his rather stern mouth was turned down at the corners. All the same, what he said was, 'Oh, indeed?' and then, 'I do hope you will give me the pleasure of your company at dinner. I'll drive you back presently.' When she hesitated he added,

'Oxford Street will be packed out with people wanting a meal after the cinema.'

A statement made at random but which reassured her. 'Oh, will it? I hadn't thought of that. We used to go to the local cinema when I was at Colbert's. Are you sure that Mrs Crib won't mind? I mean, will she have cooked enough for two?'

He assured her gravely that Mrs Crib always allowed for the unexpected guest, and began to talk gently about nothing much, putting her at her ease, and when Monty came prancing in from the garden and offered her head for a scratch, looking up at her with melting eyes, she felt all at once quite at home.

'This is a beautiful room,' she told her host. 'You must enjoy coming home to it each evening.'

It was a lovely room, comfortably large, and furnished with a nice mixture of Regency pieces and large chairs and sofas, the kind of sofas where one might put one's feet up or curl into a corner. The curtains at the windows were brocade in what she imagined one would call mulberry-red, and the thin silk carpets scattered on the polished wood floor held the same colour mixed with dull blues and greens. The walls were panelled and for the most part covered by paintings, and there was a bow-fronted cabinet along one wall, filled with fine china and silver. The fireplace was at one end of the room— Adam, she guessed—and in the winter it would hold an open fire. She gave a small sigh, not of envy but of contentment, just because she was enjoying all these things, even if only for an hour or so.

Crib came in to tell them that dinner was served, and they crossed the hall to a smaller room with crimson wallpaper and a rectangular mahogany dining-room table, large enough to seat eight people and set with lace table-mats, sparkling glass and silver. There was a bowl of roses on the table, and Florence asked, 'Are they from your garden?' and, when he nodded, 'The yellow one— isn't that Summer Sunshine? Father plans to get one for next year. I don't suppose you have much time for gardening?'

Crib put a plate of soup before her, and her lovely nose twitched at its delicious aroma. Mr Fitzgibbon studied the nose at some length without appearing to do so. 'No, I should like more time for it. I do potter at intervals, though.'

Florence addressed herself to the soup. Lettuce and cucumber, and not out of a tin either. She had quite forgotten how annoyed she had been at Mr Fitzgibbon's high-handed treatment; indeed, she hadn't felt so happy for a long time, although she didn't trouble to wonder why. The soup plates were removed, and cold chicken, salad and a snowy mound of creamed potatoes were of- fered. Mr Fitzgibbon poured white wine, passed the pepper and salt and made conversation in an easy manner while he watched Florence enjoying the meal with un- selfconscious pleasure, comparing her in his mind with other dinner companions who had shuddered at the idea of a second helping and shunned the potatoes. He frowned a little; he was allowing himself to get too interested in the girl...wanting her for his wife had been a flight of fancy.

Florence saw the frown and some of her happiness ebbed away. After their rather unfortunate encounter that evening—well, fortunate for her, she conceded—even though they hadn't seen eye to eye to begin with, the last half-hour had been delightful, but now he looked forbidding and any moment she would find herself ad- dressing him as 'sir'. She declined more potatoes politely and refused more wine. As soon as she decently could she would think of some excuse to get her out of the house, and the sooner the better.

First there was apple pie and cream to be eaten and polite small talk to be maintained. The small talk became so stilted that he looked at her in surprise. Now what was the matter with the tiresome girl? Still polite and beautifully mannered, but stiff as a poker. She responded willingly to his remarks, but the pleasant feeling that they were old friends, even though they knew very little about each other, had vanished.

They went back to the drawing-room for their coffee, and after half an hour of what Florence privately called polite conversation she said that she should be getting back. 'Mrs Twist might be worried . . .' she suggested, to which Mr Fitzgibbon made no reply, merely lifted the receiver and phoned that lady, who, it seemed, wasn't in the least worried.

'But, of course,' he said smoothly, 'you would like a good night's sleep—we have a busy day ahead of us tomorrow.'

A gentle reminder that she worked for him and it behoved her to be on duty at the right time. Or so it seemed to her.

She thanked him once again on Mrs Twist's doorstep, and later, getting ready for bed, reflected on her evening. There had been no need for Mr Fitzgibbon to take her to his home and ask her to dinner, so why had he done it? And why had he become remote, evincing no wish to hinder her from going back to her room at Mrs Twist's? She had thought once or twice just lately that they were on the verge of a cautious friendship. There was no understanding the man, she thought, punching her rather hard pillows into a semblance of softness.

In the morning everything was as usual; he arrived punctually, reminded her that his first patient was deaf, commented upon the delightful morning and made no mention of the previous evening. There was, of course, no reason why he should—all the same, she was unreasonably put out.

The deaf patient took up a good deal of time and made everyone else late, but Mr Fitzgibbon went placidly on as though the morning had ten hours to it instead of five, so that their usual lunch-break was cut short about ten minutes. She and Mrs Keane ate their sandwiches and drank a pot of tea between them, thankful that Mr Fitzgibbon had taken himself off, leaving them free to get the place straight for the afternoon patients.

'Quite a busy day,' said Mrs Keane placidly, arranging the patients' notes in a neat pile on his desk while Florence restored the examination-room to a pristine state. He returned five minutes before his first appointment and spent them on the phone to Colbert's, and after that there was no let-up until after five o'clock. Mr Fitzgibbon was at his desk, writing and being interrupted by the telephone, Mrs Keane had just made a pot of tea, and Florence was carrying a cup to him, when the waiting-room door was thrust open and Eleanor Paton came in on a wave of exquisite scent and looking ravishing in a wild-silk outfit which Florence, in a few seconds' glance, instantly coveted.

Eleanor went past her without speaking, taking the cup and saucer from her as she went, opening the consulting-room door without knocking and going inside.

'Who was that?' asked Mrs Keane, poking her nose round the kitchen door.

'Miss Paton,' said Florence quietly while she damped down rage. 'She just walked in, took his tea and went inside...'

'I'd like to be a fly on the wall,' said Mrs Keane. 'Come and have your tea, dear. Do you suppose we should take in another cup for her?'

'I don't think she would like tea-bags.'

They drank their tea and Florence, who had excellent hearing, listened to Eleanor's high-pitched voice and the occasional rumble of Mr Fitzgibbon's. There was no laughter—it sounded more like an argument, as Eleanor's tones became shrill and his became briefer.

Presently they heard the door open, and the pair of them crossed the waiting-room and out of the door, the signal for Florence to nip to the window. Mr Fitzgibbon's car was outside but he wasn't getting into it, and in a moment she saw Eleanor walking away down the street. And she didn't look round.

Florence withdrew her head cautiously and stepped back; she didn't want Mr Fitzgibbon to see her peering from his window. Her fears were ungrounded, however; he hadn't got into his car—indeed, he was standing so close to her that she felt his waistcoat sticking into the small of her back.

'Snooping?' he asked gently.

She didn't turn round but edged away from him. 'Certainly not,' she said with dignity, fingers crossed because she was telling a fib. 'I thought that you might have gone and forgotten to let us know...'

Being a parson's daughter was a terrible drawback sometimes. She turned to face him. 'No, that was a silly excuse. I looked out of the window to watch you drive Miss Paton away.'

'However, I didn't, and does that please you?'

She met his cold grey eyes steadily. 'It's none of my business, sir. I'm sorry I was—was nosy.'

'You are a very unsettling girl, Florence.' He went into his consulting-room and closed the door quietly, leaving her prey to the thought of getting a month's notice; it seemed like a strong hint that he had changed his mind about taking her on permanently. Perhaps Eleanor had persuaded him that she had been unsuitable, and she had played right into the girl's hands, hadn't she?

She went back into the examination-room, made sure that it was quite ready for the next day and then washed the cups and saucers and tidied everything away while Mrs Keane did the last of her filing. Ten minutes later Mr Fitzgibbon reappeared, bade them both a civil good evening, and went away, so that they were free to leave.

After she had eaten her supper Florence sat in Mrs Twist's small back garden; she had no heart for a walk and, since her landlady was going to spend her evening with a neighbour and had no objection to Florence sitting there if she wished, it offered a few hours of fresh air while she got on with a sweater she was knitting for her father's birthday. Not that the air was all that fresh; Mrs Twist had a neat garden, the tiny grass patch in its centre clipped to within an inch of its life, the flowers planted in rows against the low fence which separated it from the neighbours. Florence, used to a rather untidy garden with not a neighbour in sight, found the next-door children, who hung on the fence on one side, and the garrulous old man on the other side a bit distracting. However, she answered the children's questions readily enough, and when they were sent to bed entered into conversation with the old man, leaning on the top of the fence, smoking a pipe. She wondered what tobacco he used; it smelled like dried tea-leaves and charred paper and caused him to cough alarmingly. However, he was a nice person, prepared to reminisce by the hour about his youth. She gave him her full attention until he went indoors for his supper.

Daylight was fading and she let her knitting fall into her lap, finally allowing her thoughts to turn to what was uppermost in her head: the likelihood of being sacked at the end of the month. It seemed to her that it was what she could expect; looking back over the last few weeks, she reflected that she and Mr Fitzgibbon had an uneasy relationship. It had been her fault; she should never have had dinner with him in the first place—it had allowed her to glimpse him in quite a different light from the impersonal courtesy and rather austere manner he habitually wore. She went to her room and got ready for bed, and then sat up against the pillows with a pen and paper, reckoning what she should do with her salary. Even if he asked her to leave, she would have to wait until he had a replacement and they had agreed on a month's notice on either side, so she could count on six weeks' pay. Thank heaven she had got the washing-machine...

She went to work the next morning resigned to her future. It surprised her a little that she should feel so very sad, and she came to the conclusion that it was because she would be unable to buy all the things she had planned to get. Since she had felt secure in her job, the list was a long one, and now she would only be able to get a very few of the things.

The porter admitted her, wished her a good morning and volunteered the information that Mrs Keane had not yet arrived. Florence let herself into the waiting-room, changed into her uniform, adjusted her cap just so on her bright head, and went to put on the kettle. The first patient wouldn't arrive for another hour, and everything was as ready as it could be. She was in the tiny kitchen when she heard the door open. 'The kettle is on,' she called. 'Were you held up by the buses?'

She turned to see Mr Fitzgibbon, in a thin sweater and flannels, leaning against the door. 'Good morning, Florence; I've been held back by a stove-in chest.' He looked very tired and he needed a shave, and Florence, looking at him, knew why she was feeling sad: it was because if she left she would never see him again, and her heart would break because of that. Why she should have fallen in love with him she had no idea; he had given her no encouragement to do so, and why should he when he had the lovely Eleanor waiting to drop into his arms?

She asked gently, 'If you will go and sit down, will I bring you a cup of tea, sir? I'm sorry you've had a busy night.' He went away and she busied herself with a tray, thinking that she had done this once before, only then she hadn't felt as she did now. She muttered to herself, 'Now, Florence, no nonsense,' and bore the tea and biscuits into the consulting-room and found him writing.

'Must you do that?' she cried. 'Can't it wait until you've had a short sleep and a good hot breakfast?'

He put down his pen. 'You sound like a wife. Unfortunately this can't wait, but when it's done I'll go home and have breakfast and change. Does that satisfy you?'

'Oh, that isn't what I meant, sir. I didn't mean to be bossy, only you do look so tired.' She poured a cup of tea and put it beside him. 'There's Mrs Keane.'

She left him sitting there, staring at the notes he had been writing. She had made him feel every year of his age. He drank his tea, reflecting that she had never looked so young and beautiful. He had no doubt that there were other men who thought the same.

An hour later he was back at his desk, having every appearance of a man who had had a good night's sleep, ample time in which to eat a good breakfast and nothing on his brilliant mind other than his patients. Florence, ushering in the first patient, had time to take a good look at him, back at his desk, immaculately dressed as usual, getting up to shake hands with his patient, a loud-voiced young woman with an aggressive manner which, she suspected, hid nervousness. Mr Fitzgibbon ignored the aggression, examined her with impersonal kindness and finally broke the news to her that she would need to have a bronchoscopy, adding, in his most soothing manner, that if, as he suspected, she might need surgery, he would be prepared to do it. He then waited with patience while Florence dealt with his patient, who had burst into tears, followed by some wild talking. A cup of tea, a handful of tissues and gentle murmurs from Florence worked wonders, so that presently she was able to listen to Mr Fitzgibbon's plans. Showing her out into Mrs Keane's hands, Florence reflected that underneath her aggression she was really quite a nice person.

The next patient was a different kettle of fish: a thin, scholarly man of middle age, who listened quietly to what Mr Fitzgibbon had to tell him, made arrangements to go into hospital without demur and shook hands as he left, expressing his thanks for what could only be described as bad news.

The last two appointments were with children, both with bronchiolitis. Mr Fitzgibbon dealt with them very gently, making them laugh, allowing them to try out his stethoscope, making jokes. Like a nice uncle, thought

Florence, stealing a loving glance at his bowed pepper and salt head bending over one small boy.

He had a teaching round that afternoon and there were no patients until four o'clock. She and Mrs Keane ate their lunch together, and then went about their various chores until Mr Fitzgibbon returned just before four o'clock.

'Tea?' he enquired as he went into his room, but before closing the door he turned to say, 'This first appointment—the patient is a frail lady, Florence; be ready with tea and sympathy—they help a lot when it's unpleasant news.'

The little old lady who came ten minutes later looked as though a puff of wind might blow her away, but she had bright blue wide-open eyes and a serene face. Florence settled her in a chair on the other side of the desk and melted into a corner of the room until she would be needed, realising that the two already knew each other, and after a few minutes' chatting Mr Fitzgibbon said, 'Florence, Miss MacFinn was Theatre Sister at Colbert's when I was a very junior houseman—I was terrified of her!'

'Now I should be terrified of you—or at least of what you're going to tell me.' She looked across at Florence and smiled. 'Are you terrified of him, my dear?'

'Me? Heavens, no, Miss MacFinn, and I'm sure you don't need to be, although I know you're not.'

'Well, bad news is never nice, is it? I suppose you want to take a look, Alexander?'

'Indeed I do; will you go with Florence?'

So his name is Alexander, reflected Florence, busy with buttons and hooks and eyes; a very nice name and suitable. Her thoughts seemed to dwell lovingly on Mr Fitzgibbon while she carried on a cheerful conversation calculated to soothe; knowing his name made her feel that she knew something about him at last.

Miss MacFinn was philosophical about having an operation. 'Of course, if you say so, Alexander, but is it sensible at my age?'

'Certainly it is and don't cast doubts on my surgery—I'll wager a hundred pounds that you'll be trotting around on your ninetieth birthday! Will you bet on that?'

Miss MacFinn thought for a moment. 'No, I just might lose my money. You can send me a very large bouquet of flowers instead.' She looked at him straight in the eye. 'Either way!' she added.

'I'll bring them myself.' He got up, smiling, and took her hand. 'You'll go into the private wing as my special patient and no argument. I'll do it myself...'

'Good.' She looked at Florence, standing quietly by. 'It would be nice if this pretty creature would be there too...'

'I'll certainly arrange that.'

The next patient had been waiting for ten minutes or so; Florence showed him in and felt free to clear up the examination-room and get it ready once again, and after him there was only one more appointment and that was for a patient of some months, recovered from surgery and due for a check-up.

It was six o'clock before he had gone, and they began to clear up for the last time. Florence, on her way to the examination-room, was halted by Mr Fitzgibbon.

'I shall be obliged if you will make yourself available when I operate upon Miss MacFinn. I'll choose a day when Theatre Sister is off duty—you can scrub...'

When she didn't answer he added, 'Miss MacFinn liked you; we think she will need all the help she can get—even a whim satisfied.'

Florence said, 'Very well, sir,' and made for the examination-room once more, only to be stopped again.

'Get Miss Paton on the phone, will you?'

He was writing now and didn't look up.

Eleanor's voice spoke sharply in her ear. 'Yes?'

When Florence said, 'Mr Fitzgibbon wants to speak to you, Miss Paton,' she said even more sharply,

'Well, put him on, then, and don't waste my time.'

Florence handed him the receiver, her eyes sparkling with rage. She said unforgivably, 'And don't ever ask me to do that again, sir.' She swept away, and Mr Fitzgibbon, the receiver in his hand, unheeding of the voice issuing from it, grinned.

He waited until the voice paused for breath and then said quite mildly, 'I'm afraid I'll not be able to take you to the theatre, Eleanor. I'm still at my rooms and shall be for some time, and then I must go back to Colbert's.'

He listened patiently to the peevish voice and then said, 'There are any number of men only too anxious to take my place,' and with that he added, 'and I must hang up, Eleanor, or I shall be here all night.'

He was still at his desk when Florence and Mrs Keane wished him goodnight and left. They parted company on the pavement, and Florence walked slowly back to Mrs Twist's, a prey to worried thoughts. She had allowed her tongue to run away with itself again, and Mr Fitzgibbon would be justified in reprimanding her, and, if it happened that he was feeling bad-tempered, he might even give her the sack. She frowned as she opened Mrs Twist's gate, wondering why she spoke to him like that; she wouldn't have dreamed of addressing any of the patients or the consultants at Colbert's in such a fashion. She went soberly indoors, and presently sat down to sausages and mash and a pot of tea and, since Mrs Twist considered that she looked rather peaky and needed an hour or two in the air, she went obediently into the little garden and sat there, her knitting in her lap and Buster on the knitting. It was pleasant to sit there doing nothing, but a pity that her thoughts were so unsettling. 'I've cooked my goose,' she murmured to Buster, 'not that it matters, for now I have to decide whether I can bear to go on seeing him every day or whether it would be wiser to leave and never see him again. I think I'd better leave—I can say that Mother isn't so well. No, that won't do because he'll probably suggest arranging for her to be re-admitted or some such. I'll just say that she wants me at home...'

Buster rearranged the knitting to his liking and went to sleep, and Florence, closing her eyes, the better to solve her problem, went to sleep too.

CHAPTER SEVEN

FLORENCE went to work in a fine muddle the next morning; uppermost in her head was the thought that she would spend the day, or most of it, in Mr Fitzgibbon's company, but this delightful prospect was overshadowed by the memory of her flash of temper on the previous day. 'One day, my dear girl,' she muttered, 'you'll go too far and get the sack, and have to go home and never see him again.' It was really very upsetting and she dawdled along, making up conversations in her head, all of which had a satisfactory conclusion as such conversations always did.

Mr Fitzgibbon, standing at his window, staring out into the quiet street, rattling the loose change in his pocket, watched her mooning along and wondered what she might be thinking. Nothing cheerful—that was evident. He smiled to himself, studying her neat fiery head and pretty face. She was wearing a cotton dress, one of thousands off the peg, but it was a restful pale green and suited her splendid shape, and she wore it elegantly. He turned away from the window a few moments before Florence instinctively raised her eyes to it as she always did just before she crossed the street. A minute later, when she arrived, he was sitting at his desk, reading his post.

Mrs Keane, coming in on Florence's heels, wished them both good morning and wanted to know with some asperity why Mr Fitzgibbon couldn't have waited for her to deal with his letters. 'For I'm sure I'm able to deal with them far more quickly—and tidily.'

Florence went away to get into her uniform, listening wistfully to the cheerful talk between Mrs Keane and her employer—she could hear him laughing now. He hadn't even smiled at her when she had wished him good morning. Perhaps she was going to get the sack...

However, the busy day came to an end without any mention of it, and at the end of the week she went home again, reluctantly because she wouldn't see Mr Fitzgibbon until Monday morning, but happy to have a day or two in the gentle peacefulness of Gussage Tollard.

The weekend went too fast, and every hour of it had been filled. There were gooseberries and strawberries to pick, currants and some early raspberries all growing higgledy-piggledy in the untidy kitchen garden, and flowers to cut for the church. Mrs Napier, almost her old self once more, was none the less glad to take her ease while Florence took over the cooking, dealt with a load of washing and ironing and went to the village to see how Miss Payne, who had been poorly, was feeling. Well enough to give Mrs Napier a helping hand once more, Florence was assured, to her relief. Now that she had a job she had enough money to pay Miss Payne's modest wage, and the small but necessary chores she did for her mother were worth every penny of it.

In the train, going back to London, Florence mulled over her brief stay. She had enjoyed every minute of it, excepting perhaps the conversation she had had with her mother that afternoon, sitting in the garden after lunch.

'You're not quite happy, are you, darling?' her mother had remarked. 'Is this job too much for you? Is the bed-sitter too awful?'

She had denied both vigorously, and Mrs Napier had persisted gently. 'Then it's Mr Fitzgibbon—isn't he kind to you, Florence? Does he work you too hard?'

'No, no,' Florence had said, 'he's very nice to work for, Mother, and it's such an interesting job...' She had been at some pains to give chapter and verse on this, and her mother had uttered a small sigh and said no more, but Florence felt uneasy. If her mother had noticed that something was troubling her, would Mr Fitzgibbon notice it too? It seemed unlikely.

An assumption borne out by his impersonal 'good morning' when he arrived the next day. He left again as soon as he had seen his post, to go out to his out-patients clinic, for he had no appointments until the afternoon, but before he went he put his head round the examination-room door, where Florence was tidying away the week's linen.

'I shall want you in Theatre tomorrow morning. I'll pick you up here at eight o'clock sharp. I shall operate upon Miss MacFinn—if you remember, she wanted to see you again and, as Theatre Sister is on holiday, it will be most convenient.'

He had gone before she could open her mouth.

'That'll make a nice change for you, dear,' said Mrs Keane.

They separated and spent a quiet morning, doing small chores, then sitting over their coffee and finally having their sandwich lunch, so that they were ready for him when Mr Fitzgibbon returned. There were several appointments and two of them stretched into twice their usual length; by five o'clock Florence was wishing the day were over. Outside the warm day was dwindling into what was going to be a lovely evening, but, despite the open windows, the consulting-rooms were close. She envied Mr Fitzgibbon, sitting back in his chair, giving his full attention to his patients and looking cool and at ease. So he should, she reflected grumpily, when I'm the one who's doing all the running around. When the last patient finally went she carried in his tea and made for the door.

'Not so fast, Florence. Before you go I'll sort out the instruments I shall want with me tomorrow morning. Take them with you and get them sterilised at Colbert's, will you?' He eyed her quiet face over his teacup. 'A pleasant evening ahead of you, I trust?'

'Very,' said Florence; there would be shepherd's pie for supper because it was Monday, and then she would wash her hair and sit in the tiny garden and knit. Even if anyone, and by that she meant Mr Fitzgibbon, were to ask her out that evening, she wouldn't go; she was tired and cross and rather unhappy too. Not that it mattered, of course, for he wouldn't do anything of the sort.

He didn't; he reached for the phone and presently, through the half-open door, she heard him asking Eleanor if they could meet that evening.

She left with Mrs Keane after exchanging polite good evenings. It hadn't been a good day.

It was another lovely morning. She walked round to the consulting-rooms and found the Rolls outside, with Mr Fitzgibbon standing in the doorway, talking to the porter. His 'good morning' was affable, but he wasted no time in small talk. At the hospital he handed her his instruments case and told her to go on up to the theatre block. 'I'll join you in half an hour,' he told her, and walked away towards the consultant's room.

Theatre was ready; the same little staff nurse was on duty and she knew the technician and the two other nurses. She got into her theatre smock and dealt with the instruments, checked that everything was as it should be and went to the anaesthetic-room. Miss MacFinn was there, lying on the trolley, having a drowsy conversation with Dr Sim, the anaesthetist, but when she saw Florence she smiled. 'Alexander promised you'd be here. Such a treat for sore eyes you are, my dear. I've just been talking to him.'

She closed her eyes and Florence gave her hand a squeeze. 'I'll see you later,' she promised, and went to scrub up.

Everything was quite ready as Mr Fitzgibbon came into the theatre. He cast a swift eye around him, waiting while his registrar and a houseman positioned themselves on the other side of the table, asked, 'Ready, Sister?' and bent to his work.

The morning was far advanced by the time he straightened his back for the last time, pronounced himself satisfied and, leaving his registrar to apply the dressing and oversee Miss MacFinn's transfer to the recovery-room, stripped off his gloves, allowed a nurse to help him out of his gown and went away.

Miss MacFinn in safe hands, Florence took off her gown and began to gather up the instruments. She didn't get very far; the theatre maid put a cautious head round the door. 'Sister, you're to go down to the office and have your coffee. Mr Fitzgibbon says so.'

The office was crowded, with the four men perched where they could, waiting for her to pour out. Mr Fitzgibbon gravely offered her Sister's chair, behind the desk, and went to lean his bulk against one wall. She sat down composedly, gave them their mugs in turn, handed round the biscuit tin and sipped her own drink, listening to the men talking about the case. It was rather nice to be back in the hospital, she mused; on the other hand, if she were here permanently, she would see very little of Mr Fitzgibbon. She brooded over this, unaware that they had stopped talking for the moment and were looking at her.

'Hey, Florence, daydreaming? How unkind, when there are four handsome men standing around—wanting more coffee...'

She went a delicate pink. 'Sorry, I was just thinking that it was nice to see you all again.'

She began filling mugs once more, and the registrar observed, 'Which encourages me to invite you out for a meal one evening—I've no money, of course, but we can go to that poky little Chinese place...'

'I remember—they kept looking at us through those bead curtains. I'd like that, Dan.' She smiled at him; they had been out together once or twice in a friendly way; she knew that he was engaged to a girl—a children's nanny, living with a family in Switzerland—and that they planned to get married at the end of the year. Doubtless he wanted to talk about her, and Florence was a very good listener and always had been.

'Oh, good. I'll give you a ring.' He looked across to Mr Fitzgibbon, still lounging against the wall, looking thoughtful and faintly amused. 'Shall I check up on Miss MacFinn, sir?'

'No, I'll go myself, Dan. I'll take Florence back presently and come back here, do the ward-round and cast an eye on Miss MacFinn before I go, right?'

To Florence he said briskly, 'Be ready to leave here in half an hour.'

He went away and the other three men with him, leaving her to sit among the coffee-mugs and biscuit crumbs. She hadn't time to sit about, though; she went back to Theatre, saw to the instruments, checked that the theatre was ready for whatever might be coming to it next, and went away to change. Mr Fitzgibbon has said half an hour, and he wouldn't like to be kept waiting.

She got to the entrance hall a few minutes before he did, which pleased her mightily, for it seemed to her that she was always the one to be last. They got into the car without speaking, and he dropped her off at his rooms, bade her a brief goodbye and drove away. 'Home for lunch,' said Florence, sprinting up the stairs, intent on her sandwiches and tea.

There was one appointment at two o'clock and he was back at his desk five minutes before that. The patient was a middle-aged woman, quiet and composed. She did everything asked of her without demur, answered the questions put to her concisely, listened while Mr Fitzgibbon explained just why it would be necessary to have an operation, agreed to have it when arrangements could be made, thanked him nicely and went away.

Florence, putting a cup of coffee on his desk, re-marked, 'What a brave woman; I do hope she has a nice husband or children to comfort her when she gets home.'

'Indeed, yes. I am going back to Colbert's, Florence; I should like you to come with me so that Miss MacFinn can see you. Don't bother to get out of your uniform. If I'm not back by half-past five you and Mrs Keane go home.' He glanced up at her. 'Go and drink your tea— I'm leaving in ten minutes. You can tidy up when you get back.'

'How?' asked Florence. 'How do I get back?'

'I'll bring you.'

She drank her tea in a few gulps, powdered her nose and tucked away a few strands of hair, and then joined him in the waiting-room, just in time to hear him telling

Mrs Keane that he wouldn't be back until five or later and would she let anyone who phoned know this?

Eleanor, thought Florence, nipping smartly down the stairs ahead of him.

Miss MacFinn had come round from the anaesthetic and was doing nicely. She was enjoying a refreshing nap when Florence and Mr Fitzgibbon reached her room in the private wing, but within five minutes she had opened her eyes, taken a moment or two to focus them and then murmured in a thread of a voice, 'Admirably suited,' smiled faintly, and closed her eyes once more.

Florence, quite at a loss, glanced at Mr Fitzgibbon and saw that he was smiling, but within a few moments he had become the dignified consultant once again, giving low-voiced instructions to his registrar and then to Sister. That done, he turned to Florence. 'Most satisfactory,' he murmured. 'I'll take you back.'

So he drove her back to Wimpole Street and, beyond observing that Miss MacFinn had every chance of a good recovery, he had nothing else to say during the journey.

Mrs Keane, appraised of the brevity of the visit and Miss MacFinn's remark, looked thoughtful. It was strange, she reflected, that Mr Fitzgibbon treated Florence with nothing more than courteous reserve, but none the less sought her company. As pretty as a picture too, and a fine, big girl, just right for his own massive proportions, not in the least like that awful Miss Paton...

The telephone interrupted her interesting thoughts and, since she was sitting at her desk and Florence was standing by the phone, she said, 'Answer that, dear, will you? It'll be that man you rang about sharpening the surgical scissors; he said he'd ring back...'

It wasn't, it was Eleanor Paton, demanding to speak to Mr Fitzgibbon.

'He won't be back this afternoon,' said Florence politely. 'Would you like to leave a message?'

'Who's that speaking? Are you the woman with the red hair?'

Florence forgot that she was a vicar's daughter and ought to know better. 'Red hair? Brown curls, black eyes, five feet three inches tall, and slim.'

'You're new? She got the sack? Good. No, I won't leave a message...' Miss Paton hung up, and Florence replaced the receiver and looked defiantly at Mrs Keane.

'I didn't tell a fib,' she pointed out. 'If she liked to make what she wanted of it that's her business.'

Mrs Keane began to laugh. 'I'd love to see her face if ever she comes here,' she chortled.

'I wonder why she wants to see him? She sounded very cross; he arranged to see her yesterday evening—I got her on the phone for him. Do you suppose they quarrelled?'

'It must be hard to quarrel with him,' said Mrs Keane, 'it would be like butting one's head against a feather bed wrapped round a block of concrete.'

'Did he get on with Sister Brice?'

'Professionally, yes—but she wasn't his type.'

Florence couldn't stop herself from asking what his type might be.

'I don't think it's Eleanor—we'll have to wait and see.'

Perhaps, thought Florence, he had no idea himself, in which case he might remain single for the rest of his life and she would be able to go on working for him. It would be better than nothing, better than never seeing him again.

At five o'clock Mrs Keane tidied her desk. 'I should think we might go—I've got my in-laws coming to supper; I thought I'd do *coq au vin*...!'

'Then do go, Mrs Keane. I'm not in a hurry; I'll get ready to go and wait until half-past and lock up. It doesn't look as though he's coming back here.'

Mrs Keane went and Florence mooned around for another fifteen minutes. She was on the point of changing out of her uniform when the doorbell was rung. It wouldn't be Mr Fitzgibbon; he had his keys in his pocket—he'd been rattling them when they had been standing by Miss MacFinn's bedside. She opened the door: Eleanor was standing there, beating a tattoo with an impatient foot. She gave a gasp when she saw Florence. 'Why, you're still here—that other girl...' she pushed past Florence '...where is she?'

She turned to glare at Florence, standing by the still open door, saying nothing. 'It was you—there isn't another nurse.'

'I didn't say that there was,' Florence pointed out. 'I'm just locking up, and I'm afraid I must ask you to leave.'

Eleanor sat firmly down on the nearest chair. 'I intend to remain. I insist on remaining.'

They both had their backs to the door and Mr Fitzgibbon's quiet voice made them both start. He said, at his most bland, 'Go home, Florence; I'll lock up.' And when she went without a word to change, closing the door very quietly behind her, he said, 'Come into the consulting-room, Eleanor. I don't know why you've come; I think we have said all there is to say, don't you? And I'm a busy man.'

He opened the door of his consulting-room and he ushered her inside. 'That girl,' spat Eleanor. 'I phoned this afternoon; she said, well, she led me to believe that she had left—she said she was dark-haired, small and slim...'

Florence, going silently to the waiting-room door, paused when she heard his bellow of laughter. They must have made it up, she thought unhappily.

She ate her supper and, feeling restless, got on a bus and got herself taken to Colbert's. The truck driver was still in hospital and she hadn't visited him for a week or more.

He was glad to see her. His wife had just gone home and he was sitting in a chair by his bed, doing the football pools. She pulled up another chair, offered the packet of chocolate biscuits she had brought with her, and sat for half an hour, listening with her full attention to his plans for the future. No good being a truck driver, was it? he reminded her cheerfully. He'd got a bit of compensation coming to him and he was going to open a greengrocer's shop. 'And yer know wot, miss? Mr Fitzgibbon 'ad a nice little place in the Mile End Road, side-entrance and all to a real classy flat over. Said 'e was glad ter 'ave it taken off 'is 'ands, too. No rent for a year, 'e says. 'Ome in a couple of days, though I'll 'ave ter come for physio and 'ave me leg fitted.' He grinned widely at her. 'Reckon 'm lucky. The missus isn't 'arf pleased.'

'Oh, I'm so very glad,' said Florence. 'I know you'll make a success of it. Give me the address, will you? I'll come and see you.'

She took the scrap of paper he handed her and got up. 'I must go. Do take care, won't you? And I will come and see you and your wife.'

He went to the ward door with her, proud of his prowess with his crutches, and she turned and waved goodbye before she turned the corner at the end of the corridor.

She was walking along an endless corridor on her way out when Dan came through a ward door. 'Hey there, I say, I've had some splendid news—Lucy's coming back. The family she's with is coming to London; a diplomatic posting—we'll be able to see quite a lot of each other. I have missed her...'

'What wonderful news, Dan; I'm so glad. Give her my love and tell her to give me a ring, if you can spare her—we could have a good gossip.' She smiled widely at Dan and he beamed back at her, a hand on her arm. It was unfortunate for Mr Fitzgibbon's peace of mind that he should be coming towards them; from where he was, they looked absorbed in each other.

He was very near when they became aware of him, and Dan said, 'Oh, hello, sir. Have you come in about that crushed chest, or did you want to see Miss MacFinn?'

'Both,' said Mr Fitzgibbon, 'Miss MacFinn first, I think.' He slowed his pace, waiting for Dan to join him and, when he did so, nodded to Florence, smiling blandly, his eyes cold. 'Sorry to interrupt,' he said pleasantly. 'Good evening, Florence.'

The two men went away and Florence loitered along the corridor, wondering what she had done now to make him look like that—coldly angry, and with her. After all, since she'd been a member of the nursing staff at the hospital, no one objected to her coming and going at odd hours, but he had looked at her as though she had no right to be there.

She went off back to Mrs Twist's, highly incensed at his manner.

Two days went by, Mr Fitzgibbon came and went, saw his patients, dictated his letters, and addressed Florence when necessary and not otherwise in an impersonal manner which chilled her to the very marrow.

By the time Friday came she was looking forward to going home; perhaps, away from the scene of her problems, she would be able to solve them. It was halfway through the afternoon when Mrs Keane was struck by a violent migraine. Mr Fitzgibbon was at Colbert's and there were no more patients for that day; they were getting ready to go home. Mrs Keane had been lying down on the examination-room couch, but she had got up to lock her desk before she left, and the phone rang at that moment. Florence, giving the kitchen a final scrutiny, heard Mrs Keane's voice.

'I'll be there at seven o'clock, sir,' she was saying, and, 'I'll bring it with me.'

She put down the receiver and sat down limply. 'Mr Fitzgibbon wants me to go his East End clinic with some vital notes he's left here...'

'Well, you can't,' said Florence very firmly. 'Tell me where to find them and where to go and I'll take them. And I'm getting a taxi for you this very minute. You're not fit to be on your feet.'

'Oh, but I must,' said Mrs Keane feebly.

'Pooh,' said Florence, 'there's no must about it. Where is this folder?'

'You'll miss your train.'

'I'm not going until the morning,' said Florence, thinking it was quite all right and very easy to tell fibs once you got into the bad habit of it.

'You really mean that? The folder is in the left-hand drawer of his desk. It's in a blue cover and it's marked "Confidential". You really don't mind going? I don't know what he'll say...'

Florence wasn't sure either, but all she said was, 'Well, he probably won't notice. Where is it exactly?'

Mrs Keane told her. 'Not a nice district, dear. When I've been I have always had a taxi there and back. On expenses, of course.'

Florence found the folder, locked everything up and put an arm round Mrs Keane, who had her eyes shut and was looking very pale. 'I'd better come with you,' she suggested, but Mrs Keane declared that she would be all right; all the same, when the taxi came Florence begged the driver to keep an eye on his passenger and give her an arm to her front door. The cabbie was elderly and delighted to see such a pretty, charming face at the end of a day of passengers who didn't bother to look at him, only snapped directions as they got in and paid him without a glance.

'Course I will, ducks; got a bad 'ead, 'as she? My old lady gets 'em too.'

Florence said that she was sorry to hear that, and if it hadn't been for a faint moan from Mrs Keane she might have enquired further. She gave him a last smile and waved as the taxi drew away from the kerb.

Mr Fitzgibbon had said seven o'clock, and it would take quite a time to cross London, for the traffic would still be heavy. She explained to Mrs Twist, who gave her a cup of tea and a bun and promised that there would be something in the fridge when she got back, and went to her room to change. Something severe and inconspicuous, she decided, going through her few dresses. The cotton jersey, she supposed, and got into it, subdued her hair into a tidy chignon, thrust her tired feet into sandals, picked up a small handbag she could safeguard if necessary and, with the folder safely in a plastic carrier-bag, went in search of a taxi.

It was a long drive through the City, its blocks of offices silent now, the streets quiet, and then into the lighted streets of the East End, the wholesale dress shops, take-away food shops, amusement arcades, boarded-up houses and here and there high-rise flats alien to their surroundings.

The cabbie turned round once to ask if she was sure she had the right address, 'For this ain't no place for a pretty girl like you, miss.'

She assured him that she had it right. 'It's all right, it's a clinic, and I know the people who work there.'

Anything less like a clinic would be hard to find, she reflected as she got out at last, paid the cabbie, assured him that she was quite safe and crossed the pavement to the half-open door. It was a corner house, its brickwork grimed, two of its three windows boarded up, the third covered with wire netting. She turned to smile reassuringly at the cabbie and pushed open the door. The hall was dark and smelled damp, and from one of several doors there was a subdued volume of sound and a crack of light around its ill-fitting door. Florence opened it and went in.

The room wasn't large, but it was empty of furniture, save for benches against its walls and rows of decrepit chairs taking up every inch of space. It was full of people, though, and those who hadn't got seats were standing against the walls. The babble of talk died down while everyone looked at her; only the noise of the continuous coughing from some of them continued.

'Lost yer way, love?' asked a cheerful stout woman with a small boy on her lap. 'Come ter see Doc?' And, when Florence nodded, 'Well, yer'll 'ave ter take yer turn, ducks, same as the rest of us.'

'I'm not here to see him,' said Florence matter-of-factly, 'I'm a nurse, and I've brought some papers he wants urgently.'

Several voices told her to go through the door at the end of the room, and a man lounging beside it opened it for her. She thanked him nicely and went through the door on a wave of onions and beer. The atmosphere on the other side of the door was quite a different matter. What fresh air there was in the Mile End Road was pouring in through a window high up in one wall, and the walls were distempered a cheerful pale yellow. The furniture was simple: a desk, a chair behind it and another before it, an examination couch, a cabinet housing the surgery equipment, and a large sink with a pile of towels beside it. Mr Fitzgibbon was bending over a small boy on the couch, Dan was standing opposite, and beside him was the child's mother, a pretty girl with greasy hair, a grubby T-shirt and torn denim trousers. The child was screaming and kicking, and Mr Fitzgibbon had a gentle hand on the small stomach, waiting patiently until he quietened. It was a pity that the girl broke into loud sobs, and when Dan put a soothing hand on her arm flung it off and added her own screams to the child's. Florence put the folder on the desk and joined the group round the couch.

'Now, now,' she said soothingly, and put an arm round the girl's shoulders. 'Come and sit down here so that the doctors can take a look at your little boy. You can tell me all about it...'

She hardly noticed Dan's surprised stare but she couldn't fail to hear Mr Fitzgibbon's terse, 'What the devil——?'

'I'll tell you later,' she announced, and met eyes like cold steel with her own calm blue ones. 'I'll look after

Mum,' she added kindly, 'while you get on with what you want to do.'

She led the girl to a chair by a desk in a corner of the room, ignoring his tight-lipped anger. He was probably thinking some very bad language, and most certainly he would have a great deal to say to her later on. But now there was the little matter of getting the girl to stop crying. Florence produced a clean handkerchief, begged her to mop her face, gave her a drink of water from the sink tap and enquired sympathetically as to what was wrong with the child.

The girl was vague; he'd been off colour, wouldn't eat, kept being sick and said his chest hurt him. 'So I brought him here,' she explained, 'seeing as how the doctor here seems to know his stuff.'

She sniffed forlornly, and Florence said, 'Oh, you're right there; he's a very clever man.'

'You his girlfriend?'

'No, no, I'm a nurse—I work for him.'

The girl eyed her with interest, her worries forgotten for the moment. 'Got a bit of a temper, hasn't he? Doesn't show, but you can tell.' She darted a glance at the little group by the couch; the little boy was quiet now, and it was Mr Fitzgibbon talking, making the child chuckle.

He turned his head presently. 'Since you are here, Sister, perhaps you will dress this little chap while I talk to his mother.' His manner was pleasant, but his voice was cold.

It seemed wise not to speak; Florence began to clothe the child in an assortment of garments, listening as best she could to Mr Fitzgibbon at his most soothing, persuading the girl to let him take the child into hospital. He explained cystic fibrosis very simply, enquired as to her circumstances and suggested that she should see the lady at the desk in the room adjoining, who would help her to sort things out. 'I'll get an ambulance,' he told her. 'You can go with Jimmy and then stay the night at the hospital if you wish to; if you want to come back home ask the lady for your fare. Have you any money?'

He sounded so kind that Florence felt the tears crowding her throat, and when Dan came over to see how she was getting on the smile she gave him was so lop-sided that he took a second look at her, but all he said was, 'I'll phone for an ambulance.'

Mother and child were borne away presently, and Dan said, 'I'll get in the next patient, shall I?'

Mr Fitzgibbon was at his desk, finishing a conversation with Colbert's about the child he had admitted. He put the receiver down and said, 'Not for a moment. Florence, I should like to know why you are here. I spoke to Mrs Keane on the phone...'

She sat down on the chair opposite him. 'Well, it's like this—she had the most awful migraine, so I put her in a taxi and sent her home and came instead of her.' She added in a motherly voice, 'And now I'm here I might as well stay and give a hand. You're bursting with rage, aren't you? But with all these people outside there isn't really time to give vent to it, is there?'

Dan gave a muffled laugh, which he turned into a prolonged cough, but Mr Fitzgibbon didn't smile. He was in a towering rage, all the worse for its being battened down with iron determination. He glanced at his watch. 'You came by taxi?'

She nodded.

'Is it waiting?'

'Heavens, no, that would cost a small fortune, and I was told to put it down to expenses.'

'In that case you had better stay and make yourself useful.' He got up. 'Let's have the next one, Dan.'

He ignored her for the rest of the long evening, but she had little time to worry about that. Wrapped around by a white pinny she found hanging behind the door, she dressed and undressed, applied plasters, redid bandages and cleared up after each patient. The majority of them were old patients who had come for a regular check-up, but nevertheless it was past ten o'clock by the time the last one went away. Florence, helped by the quiet little lady who had been doing the paperwork and attending to the patients' problems, tidied up the place, took off the pinny and followed her to the door, nodding to Dan as she went.

'Not so fast,' said Mr Fitzgibbon, still writing at his desk. 'Dan, go on ahead, will you, and write that child up for something, and make sure his mum's being looked after? I'll be along later.'

Dan hesitated. 'Shall I take Florence with me, sir?'

'I'll take her back to her lodgings.'

Florence advanced a step into the room. 'I shall catch a bus,' she said clearly.

'No, you won't.' He didn't look up. 'Off you go, Dan; I'll see Florence safely back.'

His registrar went with a sidelong smile for Florence and, since Mr Fitzgibbon showed no sign of being ready to leave, she sat down composedly on one of the few chairs in the room.

Presently he closed the folder he was writing in and put away his pen.

'You haven't had your supper?'

'No; Mrs Twist will have left something for me.'

He got up and crossed the room to stand in front of her, making her feel at a disadvantage, since she had to look up a long way to see his face. He put out a hand and hauled her gently to her feet and didn't let her hand go.

'I have been most unkind—will you forgive me?'

He sounded so kind that she had the greatest wish to throw herself on to his chest and have a good cry; instead she looked him in the eye. 'Yes, of course I will. I must have given you a surprise. Do you like to keep all this——' she waved her free hand around '—a secret?'

'As far as I can, yes. Dan knows, of course, and so do several of the local doctors who take it in turns to work here. I've never considered it suitable for women, though.'

'Oh, pooh,' said Florence. 'What about that nice little lady who was here?'

'Ah, yes, well, she's the local school-teacher, and perfectly safe.'

She gave her hand a tug, but he held it fast. 'Well, now I know about it, may I come and work here too? I should very much like to.'

'Why, Florence?'

She had no intention of telling him why; instead she said matter-of-factly, 'It's worthwhile, isn't it? And I've every evening ...'

He lifted his eyebrows. 'Every evening? What about those evenings out with Dan?' He smiled faintly. 'A "poky little Chinese place".'

'That was years ago. I'm glad his fiancée is coming back so soon; she's a dear ...'

She glanced at him and was surprised to see what amounted to amused satisfaction on his face. 'If you want to work here I see no reason why you shouldn't, but on the definite condition that I bring you and take you back, and that you stay here in the building. I won't have you roaming the streets...'

She said coldly, 'I'm not in the habit of roaming...' and remembered the unfortunate episode when she had looked for a short-cut to the bus. 'Oh, very well. How often do you come here?'

'Once a week.' He let her hand go, picked up his bag and opened the door. 'It's getting late.'

He stowed her into the car, parked in a scruffy yard behind the house. 'I'm surprised that it's still here,' observed Florence, and then added, 'no, I'm not; they depend on you, don't they?'

'To a certain extent—most of them either need to go into hospital or have just been discharged from it.'

The streets were quiet, and the homeward journey seemed much shorter than her taxi ride.

'Mrs Twist will be in bed?' asked Mr Fitzgibbon.

'Oh, yes, but I have a key.'

'In that case there is no need to disturb her. Mrs Crib will have a meal ready.'

Florence thought longingly of food. 'Well, that's all right for you, isn't it? If you'd just drop me off at the end of this street I can——'

'Don't be silly, Florence, you will eat your supper with me and I'll bring you back afterwards.'

'I don't think——!'

'Good.' He had turned into his street and stopped before his door.

He got out, went round the car and opened her door, and said, 'Out you get,' and, when she didn't budge, scooped her up and set her on her feet on the pavement. He held her for a moment and then bent and kissed her, took her by the arm, opened his street door and urged her inside.

Since she had no means of getting back to Mrs Twist's and there was a delicious aroma coming from the half-open baize door at the back of the hall, Florence, sternly suppressing delighted thoughts about the kiss, decided sensibly to stay for supper.

CHAPTER EIGHT

MR FITZGIBBON gave Florence a gentle push from behind. 'Straight through to the kitchen. The Cribs will be in bed, but everything will be ready.'

The kitchen was roomy, with an old-fashioned dresser laden with china dishes and plates, a scrubbed wooden table in the centre of the tiled floor, and an Aga stove taking up almost all of one wall. It was flanked by two Windsor armchairs with bright cushions, and between them was Monty, roused from sleep and pleased to see them, weaving round them, uttering whispered barks. Sharing her basket was a cat, stout and matronly, who yawned widely at them and then went to sleep again.

The table had been laid for one person and with the same niceness which would have graced an elegant dining-room. Mr Fitzgibbon opened a drawer and collected spoon and forks and knives, and carried them over to the table and set them tidily beside his own place. He fetched a glass from the dresser, too, and more plates. 'Sit down,' he invited. 'I have my supper here when I go to the clinic, otherwise the Cribs would wait up. You don't mind?'

She shook her head, feeling shy because Mr Fitzgibbon was exhibiting yet another aspect of himself. Quite handy in the kitchen, she reflected, watching him ladle soup into two bowls and set them on the table. Excellent soup too, nothing out of a tin—home-made watercress soup with a blob of cream a-top and fresh brown crusty bread to go with it. After that there were chicken tartlets, kept warm in the oven, with jacket potatoes smothered in butter and a salad from the fridge. Florence forgot to be shy, ate her supper with a splendid appetite and made suitable small talk, all the while conscious of his kiss but trying not to think of it. They had their coffee presently, still sitting at the table, and he asked, 'You're going home for the weekend, Florence?'

'Yes, I promised Mother I would—we're going to make jam.' She glanced at the clock, a large old-fashioned one, hanging above the door. 'If it's convenient I'd like to go back to Mrs Twist's,' and then, by way of making conversation, she added, 'Are you going away for the weekend too?'

'Yes—like you, I'm going into the country.' He got up when she did and said, 'No, leave everything; I'll see to it when I get back.'

He drove her to her room and got out of the car and went with her to Mrs Twist's front door, took her key from her and unlocked it, gave her back her key and asked, 'Do we have to be careful of Buster?'

'No, he'll be upstairs with Mrs Twist. Thank you for a lovely supper, Mr Fitzgibbon, and...and...thank you for letting me come to your clinic each week.' She hesitated. 'But please don't think that I shall expect you to give me supper afterwards.'

'No, no, of course not, but this evening was exceptional, was it not?'

He opened the door and wished her goodnight with a casual friendliness, which for some reason annoyed her. She said 'Goodnight' quickly and went past him, but before he closed the door behind her he said, 'I do believe that we are making progress.' He shut the door before she could ask him what he meant.

Yes, there was a great deal to think about, she reflected as she got ready for bed, taking care to make no sound at all for fear of waking Mrs Twist. She got into bed and started to marshal her thoughts into sense, and went to sleep within minutes. In the morning the last evening's happenings were somehow put into their proper perspective: Mr Fitzgibbon had had every right to be surprised and annoyed at her arrival at the clinic, and common decency and good manners had forced him to take her back to his home for a meal. It was all quite explicable in the light of early morning, all except his kiss, which didn't quite fit in. She decided not to think about it any more.

She caught her train with a minute or so to spare, and sat quietly all the way to Sherborne, daydreaming; if it hadn't been for a child in the carriage excitedly pointing out the castle as they neared the little town she might have been carried on to Yeovil and beyond.

She had phoned her mother from the telephone box opposite Mrs Twist's house, and her father was on the platform waiting for her.

She drove the car back to Gussage Tollard, listening to her father's comments on the week and answering very circumspectly his queries as to her own week, and when they got home her mother, waiting with coffee and seed cake, asked the same questions, but rather more searchingly. Florence answered them all, leaving out as much as possible anything to do with Mr Fitzgibbon, something which her mother was quick to notice.

It was nice to be home; Florence pottered about the house, inspected the garden and then strolled down to the village to purchase one or two groceries her mother had forgotten.

There were several people in the shop, enjoying a gossip while they waited to be served. Florence knew them all and, after enquiring after their respective children, aged parents and whether the jam had set well, answered various enquiries as to her life in London.

'Nasty, smoky place,' observed one lady in house slippers and a printed pinny; she nodded her head wisely so that the row of curlers across her forehead nodded with it. 'No place for kids, I always say. There's Mrs Burge's youngest, went to live with his auntie and now he's in the hospital, having things done to his chest.' She beamed at Florence. 'Same as you worked in, Miss Florence—Colbert's; being looked after by a clever man, too...got a funny name—Fitz something, great big chap, she says, and ever so kind. He's got a house in Mells too; goes there at weekends...'

It was Florence's turn at the counter and she was glad of it; Mr Fitzgibbon's name, uttered so unexpectedly, had sent the colour into her cheeks and she was thankful to bend over the list in her hand.

Mrs Hoskins, serving, put a jar of Bovril on the counter and asked with a kindly curiosity, 'You'll know him, no doubt, Miss Florence? That's the smallest size Bovril I've got, tell your mother.'

'About a pound of Cheddar cheese,' said Florence and, since the village probably knew already that she worked for him but were far too nicely mannered to say so, she said, 'Well, yes, I work for him, you know. He's a very clever surgeon and marvellous with the children.'

There was a satisfied murmur from those around her, and the lady in the printed pinny looked pleased with herself. 'There, didn't I say so?' she wanted to know. 'And him living less than an hour away from here, too.'

Half an hour or so, reflected Florence silently, in that Rolls of his, and she asked for a bottle of cider vinegar, and, since he lived near by, he could quite easily give her a lift if he wanted to. Only he didn't want to.

She frowned so fiercely at the vinegar that Mrs Hoskins said hastily, 'That's the best make, Miss Florence; Mrs Napier won't have any of that nasty cheap stuff, and I won't sell it neither.'

Florence apologised quickly, adding that she had been trying to remember something or other she hadn't put on the list. Which wasn't true, but it made a good excuse. She took her purchases home presently and then went into the garden, where she attacked the weeds with such ferocity that her mother, watching from the open drawing-room window, remarked to the Reverend Mr Napier, sitting beside her, that something had upset Florence. 'I wonder what it can be?' she mused. 'Of course, it's a great help—getting the weeding done.'

Her husband, without lifting his eyes from his newspaper, agreed with her.

One of the Sunday-school teachers was on holiday and Florence had volunteered to take her place with the toddlers' class, but first she intended going off for a walk with Higgins. She was up early on Sunday morning and, with Higgins panting happily at her heels, accompanied her father as far as the church, where he was to take the early service, and then went through the lych-gate, down the narrow lane that led to Mott's Farm, and turned off over the stile into the bridle-path, which would eventually bring her out on the other side of the village. It was a glorious morning and full of the country sounds she missed in London: there were birds singing, sheep bleating, a farm tractor starting up, prepared to make its ponderous way across a field lying fallow, and then the church clock striking the hour of eight. There was plenty of time; her father wouldn't be back until almost nine o'clock, and matins would be at eleven o'clock. She sat down on a fallen log and watched Higgins gallop clumsily from one clump of trees to the other hopeful of finding rabbits, thinking inevitably of Mr Fitzgibbon.

He was at that very moment sitting in her mother's kitchen, drinking tea, looking very much at his ease with Monty at his feet.

Mrs Napier, assembling eggs and bacon and mushrooms for breakfast, had greeted him with no surprise and a great deal of inward satisfaction; it was nice to know that her maternal instincts hadn't been at fault. Here, then, was the reason for her daughter's arduous gardening, her wish to go for long walks with Higgins, her animated conversations about her week at work without any mention of Mr Fitzgibbon. She offered him tea, remarked on the beauty of the morning and volunteered the information that Florence had taken Higgins for a walk. 'Her usual early-morning round when she is at home,' she explained casually, 'down the lane to Mott's Farm, only she goes over the stile and down the bridle-path. It brings her out at the other end of the village in nice time for breakfast.'

She smiled across the kitchen at her visitor. 'Have you come far? Not from London, surely?'

'No, I have a house at Mells—do you know it? It's not so very far from here.'

'A pretty village. Of course, you'll stay and have some breakfast, won't you?'

'That would be delightful. Mr Napier is in church?'

'Yes. He will be back just before nine o'clock. There's matins at eleven, and Florence is taking one of the Sunday-school classes.'

A smile touched the corners of his mouth. He put his mug down. 'Perhaps I could overtake Florence,' he suggested blandly.

'Easily—she doesn't hurry; Higgins likes to hunt for rabbits—he never finds any, but it makes him happy.'

After he had gone Mrs Napier stood for a few minutes, her hands idle over the mushrooms she was peeling, allowing herself a few moments of pleasant daydreaming. A splendid man, she reflected, but possibly proud and reserved and liking his own way, but, on the other hand, utterly dependable and sure of himself and what he wanted. She hoped fervently that he wanted Florence.

Mr Fitzgibbon had no difficulty in finding Florence; she was still sitting on the log, her thoughts miles away, and in any case Monty had seen Higgins and rushed to meet him so noisily that she looked round to see what was happening.

Mr Fitzgibbon, walking slowly towards her, had time to admire the sun glinting on her bronze hair and the faint freckles across the bridge of her nose; he admired the colour creeping up into her cheeks when she saw him too. Her rather faded blue cotton dress and old sandals on her bare feet seemed to him to be exactly right; she was as pretty as a picture; he would have thought the same if she had been wearing a potato sack, although he had at times had the violent urge to hang her around with pearls and jewels and drape her in the very latest of fashions. He controlled his thoughts with an iron will and walked towards her and wished her a casual good morning. 'Such a splendid morning,' he continued blandly, 'and Monty needed a walk.'

Florence eyed him warily. 'All the way from Mells?' and, at his lifted eyebrows, 'Mrs Burge's youngest; they were talking about him in the village shop yesterday and someone said that you lived there.'

He sat down beside her. 'Ah, yes—Billy Burge, a delightful small boy with the heart of a lion—he's a fibrocystic...' He went on smoothly into a detailed account of the child's illness. 'He's almost well enough to go to a convalescent home—it will have to be somewhere round about here so that his family can visit easily.' He glanced at his watch. 'May I join you? Your mother said nine o'clock breakfast——'

'You've been home?'

'I had the urge to explore,' he answered smoothly, 'and I remembered that you lived here.' It seemed that was all the explanation he had to offer.

She got to her feet, and Higgins and Monty bustled up, anxious to be on the move again. 'There's time for us to follow the path round the village; it comes out at the other end of the village by the school. It's not far.'

'I dare say I can manage it,' said Mr Fitzgibbon. He sounded so meek that she gave him a suspicious look, but he was looking away from her, his face devoid of what she had suspected was sarcasm. So they walked on, slipping presently into a comfortable conversation about the country around them, the village and its inhabitants, and the pleasures of the rural life. By the time they reached the vicarage Florence was feeling happier than she had been for some time, although she had no idea why that should be. She only knew, in her mind at least, that she thought of Mr Fitzgibbon as Alexander...

They ate their breakfast in the kitchen, sitting round the solid table with its white starched cloth and blue and white china, and Mr Fitzgibbon made a splendid meal and, very much to Florence's surprise, helped with the washing-up afterwards.

She wasn't sure if she was pleased or not when her father wanted to know if their guest would like to attend morning church.

'Oh, do,' said Mrs Napier, 'and come with us and have lunch here, or if you would rather you can lie about in the garden.'

He agreed very readily to go to church, and accepted his invitation to stay for lunch.

'Oh, good,' said Mrs Napier. 'When do you have to go back to London?'

'This evening—perhaps Florence would like to come back with me?'

He looked across the table at her, faintly smiling. 'It will save you the tiresome trip across town to Mrs Twist's, Florence.'

She said slowly, 'Well, yes, thank you. But don't you want to go to your home—I mean . . . ?' She went a little pink. 'I didn't mean to be rude, but I don't want to spoil your day.'

'Oh, I don't think you'll do that. We can go there on our way back if you don't mind leaving a little earlier than usual.'

Even if she had wanted to refuse it would have been hard with her mother beaming at them both and her father observing that Sunday trains were always late and he had never liked her arriving in London late on Sunday evening.

Mr Fitzgibbon agreed quietly with him, and added blandly, 'That's settled, then. What do we do with the dogs—will they be all right while we are in church?'

'We leave Higgins in the conservatory; he's always quite happy. Monty will probably settle there too.' Mr Napier glanced at his watch. 'Florence, if you're going to take Sunday school you'd better get dressed, my dear.'

Florence went upstairs, feeling rather as though someone had taken the day away from her, rearranged it, and handed it back again. She took off the blue cotton and got into a short-sleeved crêpe dress in pale green, coiled her hair and did her face, found suitable shoes and stockings and went back downstairs, to find Mr Fitzgibbon in a tie and a beautifully tailored blazer. She frowned thoughtfully; she was sure that when he had joined her on the bridle-path he had been wearing an open-necked shirt and no tie. She caught his eye and found him smiling at her. It was a mocking smile, and it made her aware that he knew exactly what she had been thinking.

'I'll be off,' she told the room at large, and whisked herself away with a heightened colour.

Her class was large. Her father's congregation was large too, and there were a great many children in the village. She sat in the small village hall beside the church, telling them Bible stories and drawing on the blackboard to illustrate them, and at the appointed time she marshalled them into a straggling line and marched them into church to take part in the last few minutes of the service.

Mr Fitzgibbon watched her without appearing to do so, gently chivvying her restless brood into suitable quietness with an unselfconscious air which delighted him, and Mrs Napier, beside him, peeping up from under her Sunday hat, heaved a happy, hopeful sigh.

Back at the vicarage, Florence found a dozen reasons why she was unable to spend any time in Mr Fitzgibbon's company. There was the table to lay in the dining-room, the joint of beef, roasting in the oven, to inspect, its accompanying trimmings to deal with and the strawberry tart to arrange on a dish. She did all these things slowly, reluctant to join her parents and Mr Fitzgibbon, sipping sherry in the drawing-room, bewildered by the way in which he had become, as it were, a friend of the family.

'Colossal cheek,' she muttered to Charlie Brown, curled up on a kitchen chair. He flicked a lazy tail by way of answer.

She had to go to the drawing-room eventually, where she drank her sherry rather faster than she should have done and then urged her father to come and carve the joint, aware that she was not being her usual calm self and unable to do anything about it. Once they were sitting at the table, she regained some of her usual serenity and indeed she began to enjoy herself. There was no doubt about it: Mr Fitzgibbon was a pleasant companion—his manners were beautiful, his conversation interesting, and his ability to listen to other people talking and not to interrupt was unequalled. The meal progressed in a delightful manner, and it wasn't until her mother was serving her mouth-watering fruit tart that Florence looked across the table at Mr Fitzgibbon and knew in a blinding instant that she really was in love with him. The knowledge left her with a slightly open mouth, pale cheeks, a tremendous bubbling excitement and a feeling of relief that now she knew why she had been feeling so cross and vaguely unhappy.

She also realised within seconds of this discovery that on no account must anyone know about it, so that she passed plates, offered cream and remarked on the flavour of the tart in a wooden voice so unlike her usual pretty one that her mother looked sharply at her and Mr Fitzgibbon lowered his lids to hide the gleam in his eyes, watching her face as her thoughts chased themselves across her mind.

Florence removed the plates and fetched the coffee, her feet not quite touching the ground, her head a jumble of thoughts, none of which made sense. An hour on her own would be nice, she thought, but in no way was she to get it; her father declared that he would wash up, and Mr Fitzgibbon offered to help, with the almost careless air of one who always washed up on a Sunday anyway, so she and her mother repaired to the garden to sit in the elderly deck-chairs with the dogs lolling beside them.

'Such a handy man,' observed Mrs Napier, 'but I dare say he does quite a lot for himself at home.'

'He has a butler and a cook, Mother—that's in his London house; I don't know about Mells. If it's a small cottage I dare say he has to look after himself.'

'Well, do let me know, my darling—you're going there first on the way back, aren't you?' She closed her eyes. 'We'll have that Victoria sponge for tea—I wonder what time he wants to go?'

'I have no idea,' said Florence snappily. 'I think perhaps I'll change my mind and stay here and go up on the train...'

'Just as you like, love,' said her mother soothingly, 'I'm sure he'll understand.'

Florence sat up. 'Mother, what do you mean?'

'Why, nothing, darling—just an idle remark.'

The two men went for a stroll when they had done their chores, taking the dogs with them, and Florence watched them go with mixed feelings. She felt shy of Mr Fitzgibbon and anxious to present her usual matter-of-fact manner towards him; on the other hand she wanted to spend as much time as possible in his company. Sitting there, with her mother dozing beside her, she tried to decide what she should do. It would be hard to maintain that manner towards him; on the other hand if it was too hard she would have to leave her job and go somewhere where she would never see him again. She was still worrying away at the problem when they came back, and she went indoors to get the tea. Mr Fitzgibbon followed her in presently to carry the tea-tray out into the garden, casually friendly and seemingly unnoticing of her hot cheeks and stilted replies to his undemanding remarks, so that presently she pulled herself together. After all, she reflected, she was the only one who would be affected by her feelings—no one else knew, nor would they ever know. Presently, when they had finished tea, he suggested that they might be going; she agreed with her usual calm manner and went upstairs to get her overnight bag, bade her mother and father goodbye, hugged Charlie Brown and Higgins and got into the car, to hang out of the window at the last minute to call that she would be home again the following weekend. Mindful of her companion, she added, 'I hope.'

Mr Fitzgibbon was at his most urbane as he drove back to Mells; Florence, filled with a mixture of uneasiness and excitement, found herself being soothed into her usual good sense by his reassuring if rambling remarks, none of them touching on anything personal. By the time they reached Mells she had got control of herself and told herself not to behave like a silly girl; it was a situation, she was sure, which occurred over and over again, and she would cope with it.

The first sight of the house took her breath. 'Oh, how can you bear to live in London?' she demanded. 'Just look at those roses...'

Mr Fitzgibbon said mildly, 'Yes, I'm very fond of it, although I like the house in Knightsbridge too. I have the best of both worlds, have I not?'

'Well, you have really worked hard for them,' said Florence, skipping out of the car, closely observed, did she but know it, by Nanny, peering out of the funny little latticed window by the front door.

Nanny went to open the door. This one was the one, then, she reflected with satisfaction, and a nice girl too— beautiful and the proper shape. Nanny had no time for young women like blades of grass. A nice wedding, she thought cosily, and children tumbling about the old house. She opened the door, looking pleased.

Mr Fitzgibbon saw the look and grinned to himself, but he introduced Florence with perfect gravity. 'I've some papers I need to pick up, Nanny—we've had a splendid tea, but perhaps you could find us some supper before we go?'

He watched Florence's face out of the corner of his eye and saw delight, uncertainty and annoyance chase each other across it. 'It's only a couple of hours' drive— less—and I'm sure you would like to see the garden while you're here.'

'You leave it to me, Mr Alexander,' said Nanny briskly. 'A nice little chicken salad and one of my chocolate custards. In half an hour?'

'Splendid, Nanny—we ought to leave by nine o'clock at the latest.'

He turned to Florence, standing between them, feeling rather as though someone had put skates on her feet and given her a push. 'Well...' she began.

'Oh, good. Come along, then; there are some splendid roses at the side of the house, tea-roses, and some spectacular lilies—Casablanca; I put them in last year behind some Peruvian lilies.'

He led the way round the side of the house to where the garden stretched away to a magnificent red-brick wall, almost covered with wistaria, clematis and passion flower, a lawn of green velvet was edged by paths and wide herbaceous borders, bursting with summer flowers, and at the very end there was a circular bed of roses. Monty, trotting to and fro in great contentment, came and nuzzled her hand as she wandered along, very content, to admire the lilies and bend to smell the roses.

'Of course, you have a gardener?' she said presently.

'Oh, yes, but I potter around at the weekends and whenever I have an hour or so to spare.'

'Couldn't you commute?'

'I think it would be possible, but not just yet. Later, when I have a wife and family, perhaps.'

'Eleanor—Miss Paton is very pretty and wears lovely clothes...'

She had hardly been aware that she had spoken her thoughts out loud.

'Oh, quite charming,' agreed Mr Fitzgibbon placidly. 'You like clothes?'

'Well, yes, I do, but I don't have the time,' said Florence crossly and, remembering to whom she was talking, 'and of course, I don't lead that kind of life.'

'You would like to do so?'

His voice was so casual that she answered without thinking. 'Certainly not. I'd be bored stiff.' She paused to examine a rose. 'That's a lovely Super Star. Do you prune in the autumn or in February?'

They strolled round the lovely garden, Monty at their heels, talking comfortably. I'm not just in love with him, thought Florence, I like him too.

Nanny called them in presently to a supper of cold chicken—a salad, and not just a few lettuce leaves and a tomato, but apples and nuts and grapes, mixed in with chicory and chopped-up mint. There were tiny new potatoes too and a home-made dressing. They drank iced lemonade, since Mr Fitzgibbon would be driving, and finished the meal with the chocolate custards Nanny had promised them.

'I should like to thank your nanny for such a lovely supper,' said Florence, 'but I don't know her name.'

'Nanny.'

'Yes, I know that, but I'm a stranger—it would be very ill-mannered to be so familiar with her.'

'Miss Betts. Run along to the kitchen while I see to Monty. We must go in ten minutes or so.' He opened the door for her. 'It's through that arched doorway by the stairs.'

Florence trod across the hall, wishing very much that she could have seen the rest of the house; the drawing-room was perfect, so was the dining-room, but there were three more doors leading from the hall. She opened the arched door and went down a few steps to another door and, since it was shut, she knocked.

Nanny's comfortable voice bade whoever it was to go in, so she lifted the old-fashioned latch. The kitchen was at the back of the house, a large low-ceilinged room, delightfully old-fashioned but, she suspected, having every labour-saving device that could be wished for. Nanny was standing at the table, picking over a bowl of redcurrants, but she looked up and smiled as Florence went in.

'I wanted to thank you for a lovely supper, Miss Betts,' said Florence. 'And I hope it didn't make a lot of extra work for you.'

'Lor, bless you, Miss Napier, not a bit of it, and it's a treat to see the food eaten. Times I could have cried seeing it being pecked over by Mr Alexander's guests. Here he is now, come for the currants; Mrs Crib likes to make a nice fruit tart and there's nothing like your own fruit.'

Florence, aware of Mr Fitzgibbon standing behind her, agreed with her and turned to go.

'And there's no call to say Miss Betts, Miss Napier—you call me Nanny, the way Mr Alexander does.' She smiled widely. 'I dare say we'll meet again.'

To which remark Florence murmured in a non-committal way, not wishing Mr Fitzgibbon to think that she was expecting to be asked to visit his house again.

They drove away presently with Monty on the back seat, leaning forward from time to time to breathe gently into the backs of their necks.

'I expect Monty likes being in the country,' observed Florence, intent on making small talk, and, when her companion made some brief reply, enlarged upon the subject at some length, anxious for some reason for there to be no silence.

When she paused for breath, however, Mr Fitzgibbon said gently, 'Don't try so hard, Florence; your silent company is contentment enough. And could you call me Alexander when we aren't working? I begin to dislike my own name, I hear it so frequently.'

Florence stared ahead of her. Of all the rude men ... She drew a calming breath to damp down her feelings; if he wanted her silent then that was what he would get. She said stonily, 'Just as you like.' Nothing was going to make her say 'Alexander' after his remarks. Let him just wait until they were back at the consulting-rooms; if he didn't like being called Mr Fitzgibbon then she would address him as 'sir'.

'Don't sulk,' said Mr Fitzgibbon quietly. 'You have, as usual, got the wrong end of the stick.' He glanced at her cross profile. 'I fancy, however, it would be of no use putting matters right at the moment.'

They travelled some distance in silence until he said, 'I should like you to come to the hospital to see Miss MacFinn tomorrow morning. I've a round at nine o'clock; can you be ready by half-past eight or a little before that at the consulting-rooms? I only intend to look in on her for a few minutes—she has asked to see you again.'

'Very well,' said Florence. 'You have a patient at half-past eleven.'

'Yes, I'll see that you get back as soon as Miss MacFinn has had a word.' He stayed silent for a while and then said, 'I shan't see Mrs Keane before we go to Colbert's; will you ask her to change my appointments on Tuesday morning? I need to be free until one o'clock. Tell her to fit them in in the afternoon and early evening. We shall have to work late.'

'Very well,' said Florence again and looked out of the window. They didn't speak again until they reached Mrs Twist's front door, when she began a thank-you speech, uttered in a high voice quite unlike her usual quiet tones.

He cut her short. 'Oh, don't bother with that,' he begged her, 'you're as cross as two sticks, and I haven't the time to talk to you now.'

He had got out of the car as he spoke and opened her door. Florence got out haughtily, tripped up on the pavement and was set back on her feet with a, 'Tut, tut, pride goes before a fall,' as he took her arm and marched her to the door, unlocked it and, when she would have opened it, put a great hand over hers.

'I should like to think that I know the reason for your peevishness,' he observed blandly, 'but uncertainty forbids me from doing anything about it for the moment;

you are like a weathercock being blown to every point of the compass.' He bent suddenly and kissed her quickly. 'Goodnight, Florence.'

He opened the door and shoved her gently into the little hallway beyond, and just as gently shut it behind her.

Florence stood very still and tried to make sense of being called a weathercock, but she had to give up almost at once, for Mrs Twist came out of her front parlour with Buster under one arm.

'I thought I heard a car,' she observed. 'Did you get a lift back? I'm just going to make a cup of tea; have one with me—I could do with a bit of company.'

So Florence stuffed Mr Fitzgibbon and his remarks to the back of her head and sat down on the sofa of Mrs Twist's three-piece, very uncomfortable and covered in cut moquette, and gave her an expunged version of her weekend, excusing herself at length with the plea that she had to be extra early at work in the morning. 'And I dare say you're nicely tired,' said Mrs Twist. 'You'll sleep like a log.'

A remark unfortunately not borne out by Florence, who spent an almost sleepless night, her muddled thoughts going round and round in her head, so that by the time she got up she had a dreadful headache and was no nearer to enlightenment as to Mr Fitzgibbon's remarks on the previous evening and, still more important, why he had kissed her.

CHAPTER NINE

FLORENCE lay awake for a long time and woke from a heavy sleep with no wish to get up and go to work. She had a sketchy breakfast and with an eye on the clock hurried to the consulting-rooms. She reached them at the same time as the Rolls whispered to a stop, and Mr Fitzgibbon thrust open a door, bade her good morning and begged that she should get in, at the same time remarking that she looked washed out. 'You're not sickening for something?' he wanted to know with what she considered to be heartless cheerfulness.

'Certainly not. I never felt better, Mr Fitzgibbon.'

'Alexander.'

'No...'

He was weaving in and out of the morning traffic. 'No? Ah, well, it will take time, I suppose, and you're still as cross as two sticks, aren't you? Is it due to lack of sleep? It's a good thing that we have a busy day ahead of us.'

There really wasn't an answer to this, and she sat silently until they reached Colbert's and there accompanied him to the lifts, very conscious of him standing beside her as they went up to the top floor.

Miss MacFinn was sitting in a well-cushioned chair by her bed, dwarfed by the necessary paraphernalia vital to her recovery. She greeted them with pleasure and bade them sit on the bed. 'Forbidden, I know,' she chuckled, 'but no one will dare say anything to you, Alexander. I hope this is a social visit?' She smiled at Florence. 'So nice to see you again, my dear; you're beautiful, you know, and it acts like a tonic...!'

Florence blushed and looked at her feet, and heard Mr Fitzgibbon's casual, 'Yes, she is, isn't she? And a splendid worker too. So often beauty is accompanied by a bird-brain.' He got up. 'I must just have a word with Sister; I'll be back presently and run an eye over you before I take Florence back.'

He sauntered away, and Miss MacFinn said, 'Does Alexander work you hard, my dear?'

'No—oh, no, the hours are sometimes irregular, but compared with running a ward it isn't hard at all.'

'He works too hard himself. I'm relieved to know that he intends to marry. It's time he settled down and raised a family.'

Florence, her hands clasped tightly in her lap, agreed quietly, 'I'm sure a wife would be a great asset to him; he's very well-known, isn't he? And I dare say he has any number of friends and a full social life.'

Miss MacFinn coughed. 'Well, dear, I'm not sure about that; he has many friends, but if by social life you mean dinner parties and dances and so on I think you may be mistaken, although I'm sure that, provided he had the right companion, he would enjoy these things.'

'Well, yes, I expect so.'

'Tell me, have you had a pleasant weekend? You live near Sherborne, don't you? A lovely part of the country. I had friends there...'

Mr Fitzgibbon came back presently and, when Florence would have got up, said, 'No, don't go, I shall only be a moment or two.' He sat down on the bed again. 'You're doing well,' he told his patient. 'I'm going to keep you here a little longer than usual, and then you can go to your sister's. I'll listen to your chest if I may... Very satisfactory. We must be off now; I'll be in to see you some time tomorrow.'

'Thank you, Alexander, and thank you, Florence, for coming too. Come and see me again, won't you?'

Florence said that she would. 'In the evening,' she suggested, 'if that's not too late?'

She bent and kissed the elderly cheek, and Miss MacFinn remarked, 'It really is most suitable,' which puzzled Florence and brought a reluctant smile to Mr Fitzgibbon's handsome visage.

The traffic was heavy now. He didn't speak as they drove back, only when they reached the consulting-rooms he reminded her to give Mrs Keane his message about his appointments for the following day.

He had gone to open the door for her and she got out carefully, not wishing to stumble again. She said quietly, 'Very well, sir.'

Then she gasped at his sudden, 'Oh, goodness, now it's sir, is it? Back to square one.'

She paused before she crossed the pavement. 'I don't know what you mean.'

'No? Then think about it, will you? And just as soon as I have the time we'll have a talk. There's a limit to my patience.'

She gave him a startled look—the blandness of his face matched the blandness of his voice, but his eyes were a hard grey from which she flinched. All the same, she might as well give as good as she was getting.

'In that case, Mr Fitzgibbon, let us hope that you will have a few minutes to spare at the earliest opportunity.'

She sailed ahead of him, her coppery head held high, ignoring whatever it was he rumbled in reply. Something rude, she had no doubt.

There were appointments booked until one o'clock and throughout the morning he treated her with a teeth-gritting civility that she did her best to return with a highly professional manner, which, while impressive, she found quite tiring. By the end of the morning she had made up her mind. She was not a particularly impulsive girl, but suddenly the prospect of working for him, seeing him each day and knowing that he didn't care two straws for her, wasn't to be borne. When he got back at two o'clock she gave him five minutes to get settled in his chair, and with an eye on the clock, since his first appointment was barely ten minutes away, she knocked on the door and walked in.

He was writing, but he looked up when she went in. 'Yes?' He glanced at his watch and Florence, who had weakened at the sight of him, bristled.

'I'll not take a moment, Mr Fitzgibbon. I should like to leave. After a month, of course, as we agreed.'

He put down his pen and sat back in his chair. Surprise gave way to a thoughtful look from under his lids, and his smile was full of charm, so that her heart thumped against her ribs and before she could stop herself she had taken a step towards him, brought to a halt, however, by his sudden laugh. 'Splendid; nothing could be better, Florence, and you have no need to stay for a month—I'll let you off that. Go at the end of the week—we will waive our agreement.'

It was the last thing she had expected to hear. 'But you won't have a nurse.'

'I have been interviewing several likely applicants. Mrs Bates, a widow lady, is ready to start work whenever I say so.'

He sat watching her. No doubt expecting me to burst into tears, thought Florence. Well, I won't. She said in a voice that wobbled only very slightly, 'Oh, good. In that case, there's no more to be said, is there?'

'No, not at the moment.' He smiled again. 'Ask Mrs Keane to come in, will you?'

In the waiting-room Mrs Keane looked up from her typewriter. 'Florence, whatever is the matter? You're as white as a ghost. Are you all right?'

'Yes, thank you. Mr Fitzgibbon would like you to go in, Mrs Keane.'

The door was barely closed behind that lady when the first patient arrived, which was a good thing, for Florence was at once caught up in her normal routine. As the afternoon wore on it became apparent that Mrs Keane knew nothing of her departure; Florence had expected Mr Fitzgibbon to tell her, since she was privy to his professional life. She waited until the last patient had been seen and he had left to go to Colbert's, and over a cup of tea broke her news.

'Whatever for?' asked Mrs Keane. 'I thought you were happy here...'

'Well, I like the work very much—that isn't why I'm leaving. In fact, I think Mr Fitzgibbon is glad that I am going; he didn't actually say so, but he knows of a nurse who will start on Monday.'

She looked at Mrs Keane with such sad blue eyes that Mrs Keane, normally the most unsentimental of women, felt a lump in her throat. 'I'm very sorry,' she said slowly, 'and surprised. I thought—well, never mind that now. Have another cup of tea and tell me if you have any plans.'

Florence shook her head. 'Not at the moment, but I'll get another job as soon as I can—not in London, though. I'd quite like to go abroad...'

Mrs Keane, who wasn't so old that she couldn't recognise unrequited love when she saw it, suggested New Zealand in an encouraging voice. 'And the world is so small these days that distance doesn't matter any more.'

She poured more tea. She was going to miss her usual bus home, but she wasn't going to leave Florence, usually such a calm, sensible girl, to mope. 'I heard a bit of gossip this morning. Those two women—Mrs Gregg and Lady Wells, one came early and the other didn't hurry away—they were talking about Eleanor Paton—remember her? She's about to marry the owner of several factories in the Midlands—rich, they said. All I can say is thank heaven she didn't get her claws into Mr Fitzgibbon. She tried hard enough, heaven knows, but of course he was never in love with her. She was fun to take around, I suppose, and he must get lonely.'

'I'm sure that he has no need to be,' said Florence with a snap. 'The world's his oyster, isn't it?'

Florence had got back some of her pretty colour and, judging by her last remark, was feeling belligerent. Mrs Keane, satisfied, got ready to go home. Tomorrow was another day and heaven only knew what it might bring forth.

As for Florence, she went back to Mrs Twist's, ate her supper after a fashion, told that good lady that she was leaving and counteracted a volley of questions by saying simply that she was needed at home. 'Since it's such short notice, Mrs Twist, I'll pay whatever you think is fair, since you'll hardly have time to let my room before I go.'

'As to that,' said Mrs Twist, 'I was thinking of having a bit of a holiday at my sister's. She lives in Margate and I can take Buster with me.' She pressed a second helping on Florence. 'In any case, you have been a good lodger and a nice young lady. I shall miss you.' Which, from Mrs Twist, was high praise indeed.

She had another bad night and went most unwillingly to work in the morning, unnecessarily so, since Mr Fitzgibbon's manner was exactly as it always was: remote courtesy, a few remarks about the weather and a reminder that she was expected at the East End clinic that evening. She muddled through her day, gobbled the tea Mrs Twist had ready for her and took a taxi to the Mile End Road, to find Dan already there, a room packed with patients and a lady in a severe hat taking the place of the gentle soul who usually sat at the desk.

'He's on his way,' Dan told her. 'I say, what's all this about you leaving?'

'Who told you?'

He looked vague. 'Bless me if I can remember—you know how these things get around.' He gave her a friendly smile; it didn't surprise him in the least that Mr Fitzgibbon intended to marry her; he had never said so, of course, but he had taken his devoted registrar aside and warned him that he intended taking a week's holiday and that he, Dan, would have to take over his hospital work while he was away.

Dan knew better than to ask questions, but he had remarked that he and his fiancée had hoped that Mr Fitzgibbon would come to the small party they were planning before they married. 'I shall ask Florence too,' he had added, 'she's an old friend of both of us.'

Mr Fitzgibbon had fixed him with a cold grey stare. 'Florence is leaving at the weekend,' he had said in a voice which had forbidden any further remarks. Dan, however, had eyes in his head and he had seen the way his chief looked at Florence. It was to be hoped that a week's holiday would settle the matter.

Mr Fitzgibbon came in then, greeted everyone much as usual, and they got down to work. It was a long evening and the lady in the hat lacked the smooth handling of the patients so that the clinic lasted longer than usual. When the last patient had gone Mr Fitzgibbon, sitting at his desk, writing, suggested that Dan should take Florence back. 'I shall be some time,' he pointed out, 'and there is no need for her to wait.'

He bade them a pleasant goodnight and returned to his writing.

It was on Friday evening, her packing done, everything left exactly as it should be at the consulting-rooms, that Florence got on a bus and took herself off to Colbert's. She had said that she would visit Miss MacFinn, and this was her last chance.

Miss MacFinn was looking almost as good as new again. She greeted Florence with pleasure and the news that she would be going to her sister's within the next day or so, adding that she would never be sufficiently grateful to Alexander for her recovery. 'The dear man,' she said warmly, 'I'm not surprised that he's so popular with his patients. He's such a good friend too, but I expect you've discovered that for yourself.'

'Yes, oh, yes; I've enjoyed working for him, but I'm leaving tomorrow. I—I'm needed at home.'

Miss MacFinn, who knew all about it anyway, said sympathetically, 'Your mother has been ill, hasn't she? And one's first duty is to one's parents. You will miss your work, though, won't you?'

Florence said steadily, 'Yes, very much. It's most fortunate that Mr Fitzgibbon has found someone to replace me. I—I've enjoyed the work.'

'Well, I'm sure Alexander is going to miss you.' Miss MacFinn smiled at the determinedly smiling face. 'And I dare say you will miss him, my dear.'

'It was a most interesting job,' said Florence, intent on giving nothing away.

She had already said goodbye to Mrs Keane and, although she had steeled herself to bid Mr Fitzgibbon a formal goodbye, he had forestalled her by leaving unexpectedly early for Colbert's, bidding her a cheerful farewell as he went. 'I'll give you a good reference if you need one,' he had paused at the doorway to tell her. 'I'm sure you'll find an excellent job to suit you.'

He hadn't even shaken hands, she remembered indignantly.

Mrs Keane, a silent spectator, had added her own rather more leisurely goodbyes. Being a loyal receptionist and a discreet woman, she had forborn from telling Florence that Mr Fitzgibbon had, with her help, rearranged his appointments so that he would be free for the whole of the next week. He hadn't said why, or where he was going but, as she pointed out to her husband, she hadn't been born yesterday.

'We shall certainly be asked to the wedding,' she told him happily. 'I shall need a new outfit...'

Florence went home on the early morning train, bidden farewell by a surprisingly tearful Mrs Twist, and if she had hoped against hope to see Mr Fitzgibbon before she went she was doomed to disappointment. She sat and stared out of the window at the countryside, seeing nothing of it, reviewing her future. She had brought the situation upon herself, and now she had no job and would never get Alexander Fitzgibbon out of her head or see him again. It didn't bear thinking about. She began resolutely to consider her assets: a month's pay in her pocket, a row of shining new saucepans in the kitchen at home and the washing-machine, and since she was to be home for the time being there would be no need of Miss Payne's services. She thought with longing of the elegant Italian sandals she had intended to buy, and then dismissed them and concentrated on what she should tell her parents. Perhaps she should have telephoned them, but explaining would have taken some time, and anyway what had she to explain? She got out at Sherborne and saw her father waiting for her.

He saw her case at once. 'Holidays, my dear? How delightful.'

'I've left my job, Father.' She had spoken matter-of-factly but when he looked at her face he made no comment other than a remark that her mother would be delighted. 'It's such a splendid time of year to be at home,' he went on gently as he stowed the case into the car and waited patiently while Higgins greeted her.

There was plenty to talk about as they drove home—village gossip, christenings, weddings and urgent repairs to the vicarage roof. She went into the house and found her mother in the kitchen, sitting at the table, shucking peas.

'There you are, darling,' said Mrs Napier. 'You didn't phone, so we knew you'd be home.' She darted a look at her daughter's pale face. 'You look tired, dear; perhaps you should ask for a holiday.'

'I didn't need to do that, Mother—I've left my job,' said Florence bleakly.

Mrs Napier emptied a pod before she spoke. 'If you weren't happy that was the right thing to do, Florence. It will be lovely to have you at home again.'

Florence sat down opposite her mother. 'Just until I find something else. I think I'd rather like to go right away, but I haven't had time to think about it properly.'

'Well, it's nice and quiet here,' observed her mother unworriedly. 'You can take your time deciding, and a few days' doing nothing won't do you any harm.' She smiled suddenly. 'It will be so nice to have you about the place, darling.'

Florence went round the table and kissed her mother's cheek. 'One day I'll tell you about it,' she promised, 'but not just yet.'

Presently she went up to her room and unpacked her case, arranged the photos and ornaments she had taken with her to London in their original places and got into a cotton dress. An afternoon's gardening would clear her head. To keep busy was vital, because she wouldn't have the chance to think about Alexander, and if she kept busy for long enough perhaps in time she would forget him altogether. She took the pins out of her hair and tied it back carelessly, and went downstairs again to help her mother get the lunch, a meal for which she had no appetite, although she pretended to enjoy it while she talked rather too brightly about the more amusing aspects of her work in Wimpole Street. When the dishes had been washed and she had settled her mother in a garden chair for a snooze, and seen her father off to the church to see one of the church wardens about something or other, she whistled to Higgins; a quick walk before getting down to the gardening seemed a good idea.

When she got back, half an hour later, Mr Fitzgibbon's Rolls-Royce was in the front drive and he was sitting on the grass by her mother's chair. Higgins pranced forward, delighted to see Monty lolling by her master, but Florence stood stock-still as he got slowly to his feet and walked towards her.

'Go away,' said Florence, wishing with all her treacherous heart that he would stay, and then, to make things clearer, she added, 'I don't want to speak to you and, if you want me to go back and work for you, I won't.'

'My dear girl, there is nothing further from my mind.' He looked amused. 'And certainly I am going away, but first I must bid your mother goodbye.'

Which he did, before whistling to Monty, who had gone to have her ears rubbed by Florence, getting into his car and driving away with a casual wave of the hand.

'Well,' said Florence, bursting with rage and love and choked by a great lump of sadness, 'well, why did he come?'

'So kind,' said her mother presently. 'He hadn't forgotten that I had been ill and called to see if I had quite recovered.'

'Very civil of him,' agreed Florence in a colourless voice. She would telephone all the agencies she knew of on Monday and see if there were any jobs going a long way away. The other side of the world preferably.

With summer holidays in full swing and church-goers sparse, Florence found herself committed to taking the Sunday school the next morning. She was glad to do it—anything to fill the long, empty hours ahead of her. The class was a small one but unruly; she was kept fully occupied keeping law and order, marshalling the children into church for the last hymn and getting them sorted out at the end of the service. Several of them would have to be escorted to their homes in the village, and at the tail-end of the congregation she collected them ready for the short walk across the churchyard and down the village street.

Waiting for the six-year-old Kirk Pike to tie his shoe-lace, she glanced idly around her. The churchyard was peaceful, surrounded by trees and not in the least gloomy. Her father was walking along the path which would lead to the gate to the vicarage, and with him was Mr Fitzgibbon.

There was no mistaking that enormous frame. She watched until the two men disappeared from sight and then led the three small children that were in her care in the opposite direction, answering their questions with only part of her mind while she puzzled as to why he was there, talking to her father. Was he bent on getting her back to work in the consulting-rooms, and hoping to enlist her father's support? 'I'll never go back, never,' said Florence in a sudden loud voice that brought her small companions to a standstill.

She handed them over presently and walked back to the vicarage, going cautiously in case she should encounter Mr Fitzgibbon.

However, he wasn't there; there was no sign of him or his car, and she wondered if she had imagined the whole thing. But her mind was put at rest once they sat down for dinner. 'I had an unexpected visitor after matins,' observed her father, 'Mr Fitzgibbon, on his way to a luncheon party. We had a most interesting talk. He is a man of wide interests and he's interested in medieval architecture. I was telling him about the squint hole and the parvise. He tells me that there is a splendid parvise in Mells church, with a stairs in excellent preservation. He kindly invited me to visit him when he is spending a few days at his home there so that I may see it for myself.'

'How nice,' said Florence rather inadequately.

Her mother sent her to Sherborne in the morning with a list of groceries that the village shop didn't stock, and Florence was glad to go. She would need notepaper and envelopes and any number of stamps if she was going to write to all the agencies listed in the *Nursing Times*. It was a glorious day; she put on the crêpe dress, thrust her feet into sandals and got out the car.

However leisurely she was, the shopping didn't take more than an hour or so. She had coffee in a pleasant café close to the abbey, and went back to the car. Another long walk in the afternoon, she decided, driving home through the narrow winding lanes, and after that she would start her letters. New Zealand would do, she had decided, or, failing that, Canada. They were both a long way from Mr Fitzgibbon.

She took her shopping into the house, to be met by her mother bearing a large cake, covered in foil on a plate.

'Oh, good, darling. Be an angel and run down to the village hall with this, will you? It's for the Mothers' Union tea and I promised a cake. I'd take it myself presently, but old Mrs Symes always likes to cut the cakes before we begin. I don't know why, I'm sure, but one must humour old age, I suppose.'

Florence put the shopping on the kitchen table and took the cake.

'It's a snack lunch,' said Mrs Napier. 'I'll have it ready by the time you get back.'

Carrying the cake in both hands, Florence went down the hall and out of the front door. Mr Fitzgibbon was sitting on the old wooden wheelbarrow no one had bothered to move from the colourful wilderness on the other side of the drive. He had a dog on either side of him, and all three got up and came towards her as she came to a halt. The dogs barked, but Mr Fitzgibbon didn't say a word.

'Why are you here?' asked Florence fiercely. Her heart was thundering away at a fine pace and her hands were shaking so much that the cake wobbled dangerously.

He took the cake from her. 'I'll tell you as we go,' said Mr Fitzgibbon in a gentle voice calculated to soothe the most agitated of hearts.

'I don't want——!' began Florence weakly.

'Now, now, let us have no more of this. I have a week's holiday, taken at great inconvenience to myself and my patients; I have wasted two days already, and I have no intention of wasting any more.'

They were walking towards the village street; already they had passed the first of the small houses at its end, and the village hall was in sight.

'Give me that cake,' said Florence wildly.

'My dear soul, you're not fit to carry anything—you're shaking like a leaf, and I hope that it's at the sight of me.'

Florence stood still, quite forgetting that she was in full view of anyone who might be in the village shop, let alone those idle enough to be sitting at their windows looking out. She said slowly, 'Of course it's at the sight of you, Alexander; it would be silly to deny it, wouldn't it? Only now I've told you will you please go away?'

'Certainly not. Why do you suppose I've taken this holiday? Somehow the idea of proposing to you in my consulting-room didn't appeal, and on the infrequent occasions when we have been together somehow the right moment didn't occur.' He balanced the cake on one hand and took one of hers in the other. 'Will you marry me, Florence?'

She stared up at him and took a deep, glorious breath, but before she could utter they were hailed from a doorway.

'Miss Florence—is that your mother's cake? Let me have it here. I'm going to the hall now—it will save you a few steps.'

Florence wasn't listening, but Mr Fitzgibbon let her hand go and walked across the street and handed over the cake, and even spent a few moments in polite conversation before he went back to where she was still standing. He took her hand again and drew it under his arm. 'There's a little green bit between the school and the churchyard,' said Florence helpfully, and they walked there unhurriedly, watched by several ladies who had been peeping from the village shop and now crowded to the door to see what would happen next.

It was only a small green patch, but it was quiet. They stopped halfway along it, and Mr Fitzgibbon took her in his arms. 'I asked you to marry me, my darling, but before I ask you again I must tell you that I love you; I've been in love with you for some time now. Indeed, thinking about it—and I have been giving the matter a great deal of thought during the last few weeks—I believe that I loved you the moment I saw you hanging out of the window with a duster on your head.'

'But you never—never even hinted...'

'I have been so afraid that you might not love me; it wasn't until you came storming in declaring that you were going to leave that I thought that you might be a little in love with me. If you won't have me, my dearest heart, I think that I shall go into a monastery or emigrate to some far-flung spot.'

'Don't do that—don't ever go away,' said Florence urgently. 'I couldn't bear it. It took me quite a while to discover that I loved you, but I do and I shan't change.'

Mr Fitzgibbon swept her into his arms. 'I'll see that you don't.' He kissed her then, taking his time about it, and then he kissed her again.

The small green patch was no longer quiet; the village school had let its pupils out for their dinners, and a row of interested faces was watching them over the wall.

''E's kissing and cuddling our Miss Florence,' said a voice. Then there came a shrill, 'Hey, mister, will you get married?'

Mr Fitzgibbon lifted his head. 'That is our intention. Why not go home and tell everybody?'

Florence lifted her head from his shoulder. 'Alexander...'

'Say that again.'

'What? Alexander? Why?'

'It sounds nice...'

She smiled. 'Alexander, darling,' said Florence, and kissed him.

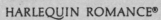

HARLEQUIN ROMANCE®

**Harlequin Romance
makes love
an adventure!**

Don't miss
next month's
exciting story in

THE BRIDAL
COLLECTION

RESCUED BY LOVE
by Anne Marie Duquette

THE BRIDE wanted a new future.
THE GROOM was haunted by his past.
THEIR WEDDING was a Grand affair!

Available this month in
The Bridal Collection:
A BRIDE FOR RANSOM
by Renee Roszel
Harlequin Romance #3251
Wherever Harlequin books are sold.

WED-11

Where do you find hot Texas nights, smooth Texas charm and dangerously sexy cowboys?

DEEP IN THE HEART

Wedding Bells—Texas Style!

Even a Boston blue blood needs a Texas education. Ranch owner J. T. McKinney is handsome, strong, opinionated and totally charming. And he is determined to marry beautiful Bostonian Cynthia Page. However, the couple soon discovers a Texas cattleman's idea of marriage differs greatly from a New England career woman's!

CRYSTAL CREEK reverberates with the exciting rhythm of Texas. Each story features the rugged individuals who live and love in the Lone Star State. And each one ends with the same invitation...

Y'ALL COME BACK...REAL SOON!

Don't miss *DEEP IN THE HEART* by Barbara Kaye. Available in March wherever Harlequin books are sold.

**Harlequin is proud to present our
best authors, their best books and
the best for your reading pleasure!**

Throughout 1993, Harlequin will bring you
exciting books by some of the top names in
contemporary romance!

In February,
look for
Twist of Fate by

Hannah Jessett had been content with her
quiet life. Suddenly she was the center of a
corporate battle with wealthy
entrepreneur Gideon Cage. Now Hannah
must choose between the fame and money
an inheritance has brought or a love that
may not be as it appears.

Don't miss TWIST OF FATE ...
wherever Harlequin books are sold.

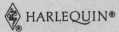

HARLEQUIN®

my Valentine

1993

The most romantic day of the year is here! Escape into the exquisite world of love with MY VALENTINE 1993. What better way to celebrate Valentine's Day than with this very romantic, sensuous collection of four original short stories, written by some of Harlequin's most popular authors.

**ANNE STUART
JUDITH ARNOLD
ANNE McALLISTER
LINDA RANDALL WISDOM**

THIS VALENTINE'S DAY, DISCOVER ROMANCE WITH MY VALENTINE 1993

Available in February wherever Harlequin Books are sold.　VAL93